Slithering Menace

A collection of short stories by J.P Renehan

This novel is entirely a work of fiction. The names, characters and incidents portrayed in it are the work of the author's imagination. Any resemblance to actual persons, living or dead, events or localities is entirely coincidental.

J.P Renehan asserts the moral right to be identified as the author of this work.

Designations used by companies to distinguish their products are often claimed as trademarks. All brand names and product names used in this book and on its cover are trade names, service marks, trademarks and registered trademarks of their respective owners. The publishers and the book are not associated with any product or vendor mentioned in this book. None of the companies referenced within the book have endorsed the book.

ISBN: 9781797600567

JUB'R

This piece of information appeared in a discussion forum on font creation online and was dated 12th of July 2006. The long post had been uploaded by a user called "Jub'rDance" whose IP address traced back to Parkgate, Wirral England.

I worked as a website designer then. It was easy to find clients to pay me, not many people did what I did for a living. I could work when I wanted and where I wanted.

I was building a site for a local historical society, a stuffy collective of flapjack eating imbeciles to my mind, but I enjoyed the prospect of writing copy that was far away from the tiresome business speak that I was forced to use and the same, tired colours and photographs for the same, tired looking sites that people wanted.

The sage green and light browns of the buttons and sidebars evoked a feeling of history; an impression of wood panelling and chesterfield suites. The fonts I had chosen however were poor. They seemed flat in comparison to the work I had put in to the graphics of the pages. Not one of the options I had come across in my editing suite were suitable and I had taken the time to browse through the many fonts available online. I had chosen two but only because they were the least ill at ease with the site I was building.

After my evening meal of some hot buttered toast smothered with jam and strong tea I sat back at my desk and looked across the room to my bookcase. My mind was numb after a long time in front of my monitor and the books on the shelves seemed stimulating with their bold titles and non-prosaic names. PSYCHOPATHOLOGY OF A KILLER, SERIAL MURDERS: EVIDENCE FROM THE LABORATORY, THE RIPPER ENCYCLOPEDIA; all seemed much more interesting than the search for a boring font for a boring website. I decided to take a book to bed and sleep on the design issue. Before shutting down the PC I went on to a favourite forum and placed a request for anyone who had ideas for a font that would be suitable for a historical and archaeological site design.

I dreamt that night of a wall, barely discernable in the darkness, beyond which came a shuffling and scraping. My breath was forced and uneven with fear as I frowned to hear the sounds closer, my trembling hand reached out to touch the dirty, pitted bricks and crumbling mortar but would go no further toward the wall out fear, despite my will's insistence.

It had just gone past 5AM when I awoke and was still dark.

My hands were still shaking as I gripped my coffee and watched the screen come to life. Huddled in my office chair in my dressing gown waiting for the heating to take the chill off the room. I checked my emails, nothing, and then thought a browse on the internet might be settling before getting showered and dressed. The idea of going back to sleep, even at this time on a Saturday morning, was inconceivable after that odd dream.

There as a reply to my request on the forum, a user named YGc had posted a link to a zip file called Jub'r and a short message, "say his name or write his words".

It was slightly cryptic but, this was the internet and at least someone had shown an interest.

I scanned the file for a virus and then opened it. A True Type font file named Jub'r was the only thing there. It was safe to use so I went ahead and installed it. Opening up my word processor and selecting the font I noticed the Jub'r font appeared at first to be some form of Arabic, it certainly did not seem to be a Latin font from the initial view in the font preview window that was open. I selected it and typed "and" into the application. The font appeared on the screen and seemed indecipherable at first, then on a second look I could see the word "and". The A was twisted in a strange way that suggested calligraphy or a twisted ribbon of paper, the N was inverted like the Arabic and the D was a number of twisted bands of lines that spilled across each other in a never ending series of swirls. I narrowed my eyes and looked at the letters as they seemed to flicker and move through a range of colours on the screen. I looked down, away from the screen, at my coffee and smelt a metallic scent or taste of blood, my hands were sweating and my temples throbbed, pounding through my ears. I wiped at my mouth with the back of my hand and drew it away covered in blood that was running from my nose. I avoided the screen as I pinched my nose and tilted my head back to stare at the ceiling. My little dogs yapped. The renewed clarity in my mind was helped on by the hot shower I had taken, the clean clothes and the third strong cup of coffee that morning. The drizzle was coming down in sheets outside the bay windows but it was warm and comfortable inside. I could just make out the cars on the main road a way away spraying

water as they drove past the quiet side road I lived on. I couldn't even hear them thanks to the double glazed windows. I moved forward and pulled back the net curtain, looking down at the window. It was odd but the PCs monitor had come out of standby and was reflecting in the window. The word AND in that font was clearly visible in the window with the rain coursing behind the letters and down the pane.
PAIN.
I put the coffee down on the window ledge and walked to my PC slowly, my twitching hands slowly moving their fingers back and forth involuntarily. The font seemed to call to me, drawing me to the screen, to the computer and to the folder I had hidden on there. The folder only I knew about. My special folder.
I sat down and navigated to where the hidden folder was kept and unlocked it. It flashed open and a shiver shocked down me and into my being. Myriad moments of torture and suffering. Videos, drawings, photographs, even snuff films I had spent so long acquiring on the deep web.
Jub'r
I typed the word PAIN into my word processor and the font came alive, almost burned out of the screen with a ferocity that drew a short breath through my teeth. A jumble of confused letters cascaded together and then fell apart. The images flashed into my mind, the wall, the screams, the suffering. I turned my head to look once again at the books on my shelf; SERIAL KILLERS OF NORTH AMERICA. My mind raced, I felt uncertain of exactly where I was. I seemed to turn but might just as easily have simply lay upon the desk, as I awoke sometime later.

It was dusk and the only illumination in the room was the PC's monitor which had failed to go on standby again. The word processing application was still open and beneath the word PAIN was typed the word Y'GOLONAC. It flashed; the Jub'r font displayed its sickening, terrifying *sound* with a macabre precision. The sight of the word seemed almost *audible*.

Why had I typed that?

I lifted a hand to turn off the monitor. It was caked in dried blood. Damned nose must have been bleeding again.

I lifted myself up and lay down on the sofa.

Why would I type Y'GOLONAC? Why would I type his name? How did I know it was someone's name?

I looked at my bloodied hand and the sweat that dripped across my palm from between my fingers. As the moisture followed the creases of my skin it created a lighter seam that flushed the ochre away. I could almost see a mouth there. An obscene, glistening mouth that opened and closed as I drew my fingers back and then forward.

I grinned at it and closed my eyes.

In my ears was the sound of panting, the quick rasps of breath caught through exertion. The sound of wailing and screaming. It felt exuberant, mesmerising. The feel of dust and the cold slate floor beneath my slipping feet. Was I dancing? Running?

Then it stopped.

There was a wall. Bottle green tiles, oblong and laid side down adorned the wall to its halfway point, then a line of ornate brown dado tiles on top of which the bare plaster had been painted in a nicotine coloured cream. The thing looked Victorian, institutional. Yet it seemed to almost breathe. I could see the centre of the wall expand and contract very slightly with a wheezing regularity.

I backed away appalled and yet intrigued by the malevolence behind that wall. Something unspeakable hid behind there. I moved quickly but chaotically as I fled from that wall, passing corridors similarly adorned, fire doors that lay ajar, unused.

It was a school, here was a classroom with its door open. The wooden desks with their hinged lids, the wooden chairs with their rounded ages from years of use. The smell of must and mould of a place that had sat unused for years.

Yet no graffiti, as cold and damp as a ruin but not a thing out of place. No smashed windows, high up in the walls though they were. No doors but for the one I stood outside and the fire doors. A twisting corridor that led from something terrible to an unknown destination.

The howling started again. This time filling the corridor with its roar. I backed into the classroom and pressed my hands to my ears. He could see me, hear my heart pounding. He knew I was here and waited for me. Y'Golonac, the Defiler, the taster of flesh. Served by his blind, shrouded minions and waiting for the next moment to feed his open, gnarling maws. Insensate and insatiable. The glistening, fang toothed mouth set into the palm of each hand. The obscenely long and serpent-like tongue which flailed and stretched as if searching, hunting.

The noise echoed around the classroom, there was no escape in this place. The bottle green walls seemed to blast the screeches across the room like the ricochets of

bullets. I left the classroom and moved away, down the corridor in the first direction my feet would take me.
I could see it now in my mind, the bloodied stump where the head should be, the twitching neck stem and the glistening gore that topped it. Yet, Y'Golonac survived, never seeing, only knowing. The mouths in his hands cackling and snapping as his obese, yellowed torso plodded here and there in the darkness behind that wall. Waiting, patiently waiting and knowing.
I could see his name now in Jubr; finally the swaying and throbbing of the word made sense. It was a carnal dance made into communication. A calling to the utter destruction of the mind and then the very being. The call to give oneself to the great one, the most horrifying Y'Golonac. To be defiled and rent asunder. Rent asunder as I had done to those animals, the blood on my hands, their screams. The laughing, howling. The cries of pain and pleading from the sights I had watched and obsessed over. All was here now; displayed before the mighty Y'Golonac.
As the thing roared its triumph and the rolls of its fat cascaded down to its hanging, withered genitals my feet joined the throng. Joined the screaming and pleading in maddened words that made no meaning. Naked now and stumbling; eyes gone, taken for the feast of the great one, arms ripped away by the maws to leave bloodied stumps that waved to keep what was left of myself upright.
Reeling, spinning with the others. A blasphemous sight and then a bloodied oblation to that obese abortion.

Dark Young

D.I Ardwood Stayves looked out of the Ford Granada's window; only partially rolled down to let out the pea-souper of tobacco smoke from his heavy habit.

"You sure about this Davis? It's in the middle of bloody nowhere"? He gestured with his head, over the stile, towards the woodland, a short distance away.

"It's what it says here, guv. Local dog walker found it first thing this morning", replied Davis looking at the pieces of A4 he had balanced against the steering wheel.

"Thought no one came into these woods 'cos of all the pervs and poltergeists"?

"Apparently this fella does, whenever it's clear and not raining. According to his statement he never spotted the thing before, it's only 'cos the brambles had been crushed down and ripped up he saw it". Davis folded the papers up and pressed them into the pocket of his suit jacket.

"We having a look then guv"?

"That's the thing about letting kids like you into the C.I.D son, you're far too bright and cheery at this time of day. I should be sleeping it off from last night, not traipsing around a field full of dogshit at half eleven in the morning". Stayves got out of the car groaning and attempting to straighten his crooked tie.

Davis had to admit his boss was right. With the stubble, greying hair in need of a comb and eyes like a demon he did not look well after his usual night on the town.

"Perhaps you should sit in the car guv? I'll go and take

a look"?
Stayves cast him a withering look.
"Shut up Detective Constable and show me where the bloody thing is", he reached into his breast pocket and retrieved another cigarette. He was made to be in the grimy town he was used to; not here in this weird place full of twittering birds and air that smelt of, well, the countryside.
Davis was out of the car and looking at a small, green Austin Allegro that was parked beneath some elms on the far side of the small layby that operated as a car park.
"Oi, guv, that car's scene of crimes isn't it".
Stayves followed Davis' outstretched finger and his narrowed, watery eyes located the Allegro parked in the heavy shade.
"Oh, bloody hell. That's all we need. Dr Jekyll and Mr bloody Hyde." He lit his cigarette and threw his match down after shaking it out. "C'mon Constable, mustn't keep the brainies waiting".
The area they were here to investigate was only a few hundred yards from the stile. It was immediately recognisable, not only due to the torn up and flattened foliage but also by the flimsy piece of tape that had been stretched across the area with;
POLICE LINE. DO NOT CROSS
Written on it.
"Looks like someone's trying to keep us out guv".
"Yeah, and bloody advertising the place while they're at it. They might as well hang up some chuffing tinsel and bloody fairy lights while they're at it", Stayves lifted the tape and walked underneath it.
"Police line, do not grotto, eh, guv", DC Dan Davis

chuckled to himself.

"Shut up Constable, my sides can't take any more mirth this morning", Stayves pressed on and soon came into a sizeable dell that seemed to appear out of nowhere in the tangled brambles and ferns. Immediately noticeable were the burnt patches of grass, grass which had been pounded flat; almost as if rows of tents had been pitched upon them for a few days. The object in the centre of the glade drew the most attention though. A long, needle like stone stele. Carved with mysterious symbols, caked in a brown stain at the base and rising to a seemingly sharp tip at the top.

Next to the stele stood a tall, wiry man, almost a stele himself. Dressed in brown flared slacks and a green nylon packamac, with huge pocket, he almost blended in to the flora. He was busy taking photographs of the base of the obelisk and mumbling to himself.

"That's that scene of crimes bloke that came in to the office a couple of weeks ago to introduce himself", Davis nodded towards the man.

"I don't remember him", Stayves wrinkled his nose and furrowed his brow.

"Nah, you went off to the pub with that bird June from the betting shop".

"Oh, yeah. Flaming June. What a bloody Tuesday that turned out to be", Stayves drew heavily on his cigarette and shook his head.

Davis walked forward and raised his hand, waving it at the man.

"Eh, Trevor. It's me".

The man looked up, blank faced for a moment before letting out a beaming smile.

"Detective Constable Dan Davis. How are you"?

"Sound as a pound mate. This is my D.I; Trevor Marks, meet Detective Inspector Ardwood Stayves"

Stayves snorted.

"Marks? You're a forensics officer called Marks? You're having a laugh aren't you"?

"With a name like Ardwood Stayves I wouldn't be throwing stones Inspector", replied Marks.

"Too, bloody, chay", Stayves responded moodily.

"Found anything then"? Said Davis.

Marks turned and nodded, placed his camera down carefully and picked up some clear ziplocked bags. The first one he held up had two small items that looked like pearls.

"Two teeth, definitely human, one incisor and one canine. Judging by the size of them I'd say they came from a young teenager."

Stayves winced, he hated hearing this kind of news. He took his cigarette out of his mouth and dropped it onto the grass, twisting his shoe on it to stub it out.

"May I remind you this is a crime scene Inspector", Marks frowned for a moment but the steel, icy stare from the Detective Inspector stopped him taking things any further.

"This next sample is from the brown residue at the base of the stele"

"The what"? Asked Davis.

"The stele Dan", Marks grinned inwardly, "It's what these tall, oblong obelisks are called".

"And the brown stuff"? Stayves nodded at the base of the stele.

"Almost certainly blood. I have a sample of scrapings here for testing. We won't know what type it is until the boffins at the uni do a lab test".

"Have any clue on what those carvings say on the stone Trev"? Davis leaned in to take a closer look.
"They look like cuneiform" Stayves interjected blithely.
"What the hell guv, how do you know that"? Davis looked genuinely stunned.
"I saw it in a book at the barbers about aliens coming down and building the pyramids. It's an ancient form of handwriting".
"So this thing has probably been sitting in the middle of all these trees for hundreds of years and no one has ever seen it until now"? Davis backed away slightly.
"I doubt it", said Marks flatly.
"You think this place was open to people seeing this a few hundred years ago. These woods aren't that old"? Stayves looked around the glade at the mostly silver birch trees.
"No, I just don't think the thing itself is that old". Marks replied.
"Why"?
"Because it's cast out of concrete".
"What"?
"Because it's made out of concrete".

Chapter 2

"Let's get a bacon butty Davis. I can do without this crap today", Stayves grabbed the passenger side ceiling handle as the Granada sped away from the crime scene. Not ten minutes later Stayves was sitting with his legs splayed out of the vehicle resting his arm on the frame of the rolled down window. He was finishing his cigarette as Davis arrived.
"Bacon butty and a strong cuppa with no sugar guv".
"Cheers Dan, I'll get the next one".
He bit into the sandwich and began mulling over the bizarre idea that an ancient monument might actually be something modern, cast out of concrete. Why? Who would make something like that? The woods backs on to a council estate. It's not like there are gangs of middle class artsy people types that would just plonk something like that out in the woods.
There had to be a reason. Stayves thought of the modern druids down at Stonehenge. Not the same, they were modern weirdoes in bed linen standing around ancient stones. This is a cast, concrete stone, deliberately hidden from sight. How had no one ever spotted it or no dog ever sniffed it out?
""Should've got an egg too; brain food. All that protein", said Stayves.
"That's why that suit's becoming too tight guv", Dan nodded at his DI's waistline.
"My suit doesn't fit because I spend all my time sitting in this car eating pasties and bacon sandwiches with you".

"Maybe that's what happened to your hair guv? Your head got so big your hair doesn't fit anymore"?

"Yes, very droll Constable, very dry. Now put that in the bloody bin will you"? He swigged down the last of his tea, crumpled up the wrapper of his bacon sandwich, stuffed it in the Styrofoam cup and threw it for Davis to catch.
"You got that OS map in the car"?
"In the glove box guv".
Stayves traced a line with his forefinger where they had driven along the main road to where the woods were. He was surprised at just how much open land there was around the location. When you were sat outside Rod's hot dog and breakfast butty caravan on a busy main road it was hard to believe there were fields and birds and that fresh air stuff only a few miles away. The woods backed on to the large Council Estate as Stayves had presumed. The rest of the area was made up of riding stables, a few small farms, an industrial estate and a few scattered houses for the semi well-to-do.
He had heard from uniform that the estate was getting a bit of a reputation for itself. He'd only been there a few times, initially to follow some leads from town but on the last couple of times it had been as part of drugs raids and an arrest for serious assault and possession. The place had changed beyond all recognition in the last few years as it was used as a dumping ground for migrants that couldn't be housed elsewhere. Those that could not or would not speak English, those whose behaviours would be an assault to the sensibilities of the same people that brought them over.

There were plenty of tales of whole families living in two up and two downs; sometimes twenty people. Where the fixtures and fittings had been removed and sold off. Some places where uniformed officers, even in their panda cars, thought twice about visiting.

Davis bundled himself into the car.

"We going orienteering then guv"?

"I see that cup of tea's filled you with energy then Davis. Better make sure we make use of that before your afternoon nap. Get your foot down. I want to see a man about a dog".

The tyres screeched on the tarmac as the Ford Granada hot rodded from Rod's hot dogs.

The Moyer Park estate was built in the late forties to rehouse people from the slums of the bigger towns on the edge of the Mersey. For the past decade it had been falling into a spire of drugs, street violence and unemployment. For many on the estate they would live and die in its environs, rarely setting foot outside its fences and walls.

The Granada tooled along the pitted tarmac road at a slow pace, its occupants looking increasingly at odds with its surroundings. Here and there groups of new arrivals to the country would stop conversing in their tongue and turn to look at the obvious policemen that were driving by.

"This is ridiculous Davis. Bloody ridiculous".

"Lucky we're only heading into the outskirts guv. If we were going into the centre of the estate then we'd be in serious trouble".

The car pulled up outside a plain looking two up two down semi-detached house, tan coloured bricks and badly painted wooden windows. A dog inside began barking as they exited the car banging the doors. A well maintained, blue Vauxhall Chevette was parked on the road outside. A small group of onlookers were assembled at the entrance to the cul-de-sac, the women wearing headscarves and all silently watching the proceedings.

Stayves rapped at the door, first politely then harder as the dog's barking got louder.

The door opened partially after some fumbling with multiple locks and an ashen face peered over the security chain that limited the door's opening.

"What do you want"? The accent was local but hushed, this man was fearful.

"I'm Detective Inspector Stayves and this is Detective Constable Davis. Is there any chance we could come in and talk to you about the stone pillar you found this morning"?

The door closed and the chain batted against the door as it was freed from the sliding lock. Faint mumbling could be heard from the man as the door opened to let them in.

The Alsatian sat behind his master regarding the two policemen with a confused glare.

"I've had two officers around this morning already", the man was visibly nervous. "I'm supposed to be at work".

Stayves loosened his tie a little, he knew he'd get into trouble for jumping the gun again and interviewing this witness before he'd seen the report from uniform.

"Just a couple of things Mr"? Stayves nodded to Davis to begin taking notes in his pad.

"Mr Smethwick, Roger Smethwick".

"So Mr Smethwick, you are a regular walker in the

woods over there"? Stayves gestured with his head toward the crime scene not half a mile away.

"No, I never really go there, I was running late for work this morning and just took the dog out for a quick run on the way to get some milk from the shop before heading off to Hero Tyres, where I work like. I normally walk him alongside the golf course by the motorway."

"So you've never seen that stone pillar before"?

"No, the dog went ballistic when he got on the path, just ran off. He started barking at the trees and then when I got near him he ran off into the brambles and stuff that had been all torn up and flattened. It was only when I saw that stone thing that I thought anything weird was going on.

I got back in the car, drove back here and phoned the Police, you lot, as soon as I got in. Wish I hadn't now. There's bound to be trouble after you lot keep calling round every hour or so". Smethwick gestured out of the window where the same group of onlookers where now outside the front fence, some trying to see through the net curtains and others regarding the Ford Granada with considerable suspicion.

"So you didn't see anyone or hear anyone moving whilst you were in the area? No parked cars? No other dog walkers"? Stayves checked his watch.

"Nothing, it was completely quiet".

"And everything was quiet on the estate last night was it? No noise or shouting or anything"?

Smethwick looked back blankly. "No, nothing".

"Well we won't be bothering you further Mr Smethwick, not unless we need you", Stayves gestured to Davis to close his notepad and then stood up to leave.

"Take this, if you need to speak to me my office number is on it. There'll be someone to take a message for you no matter when you call". He handed one of his cards to Smethwick who looked at it with suspicion. The onlookers moved on as the door opened, dispersing across the cul-de-sac like startled birds. Odd, as there was no birdsong in the entire place. Maybe that's why that woods had seemed so alien and unwelcoming?

As the car left the estate and began moving up the gentle slope toward the motorway, past the entrance to the woods they had parked at earlier, Stayves became edgy. He'd never felt quite this alarmed for no reason before. He was used to feeling a certain intuitive unease when things didn't add up or something was gnawing at him. That much was part and parcel of being an experienced D.I. No, this was much more visceral. Almost like a panic attack.

As the car moved past the entrance to the woods three figures stood, motionless. Two of them in their teens, swarthy and hair as dark as jet, both of the same ilk as the onlookers on the estate. Both male teens looked at the car nonplussed as it moved past. The other creature Stayves took to be a dog attached to a lead. As the car joined the motorway he furrowed his brows and looked back. That dog had horns, he could swear it. That was a goat, not a dog surely?

Chapter 3

Back at the station's cramped, untidy office Stayves was reassured by the bustle and constant noise of his fellow detectives. Reams of paper were stacked on most of the tables and phones were ringing all thanks to a major restructuring in the offices.
Penpushers' work.
As if on cue the shiny pate and aquiline nose of his superior entered through the main office door.
"Here we go Davis; old chrome dome come to give me a good rollicking".
Davis looked over to the main door and groaned.
"Tell you what, you have a shufty around and see if you can get any info on where that pillar might have come from; try local builder's yards, stuff like that. Probably look for people that don't look like they belong on a building site. I'll deal with his nibs here".
"Will do Guv, good luck", Davis exited the office at some pace.
"DI Stayves, mind if I have a word"? His superior was calm as usual.
"Of course guv, there's a free office in here", Stayves frowned, he knew what was coming, it was a weekly occurrence.

By the time Stayves got back to his flat it was starting to get dark, it was an evening ritual to round off a day's work with a few ales at the local. The familiar stumble up to the first floor after a couple of pints seemed to lend a reassurance to the other tenants that the law had arrived. The television sets would lower in volume as he opened the main door and then return to their previous volume once Stayves began to ascend the stairs.

His flat was a mess, there were no cushions on the settee, only a blanket and three pillows. The coffee table was a repository for empty fag packets, a mountain of cigarette butts in a stolen pub ashtray and a few empty bottles of cheap whisky.

He switched on the television set and waited for it to warm up. Kicking his slip on shoes onto the floor, taking off his still tied tie and throwing his grey jacket onto a nearby chair. He reached into his trouser pocket and pulled out an unopened half bottle of whisky, a memento of the Farmers Arms public house.

With cigarette lit and his now cleaned glass (care of the blanket) topped up with whisky he was pleased that News at Ten had started at exactly the perfect time; the familiar peels of Big Ben tolling from the crackly speaker.

Stayves leant back on the sofa, toasted the television and then rested his glass on his belly.

Sleep never came easily for him. There was a lot for his mind to process from the day, it didn't help that he habitually crashed out, semi-clothed on his sofa.

Oddly enough this time he fell asleep almost as soon as his eyes had closed.

He was on a narrow, chalk track; crested on each side by grey, dusty grass and worn and badly kept green mesh and concrete post fencing. Beyond the fence, and meeting to form a canopy, were many large trees. Their boughs twisted amongst one another like some living, Celtic knot work.

The whole scene was tinged with an ethereal purple glow that made the hair prickle on Stayves' arms. It should have been something of a serene scene but somehow the whole vision seemed spoiled, somehow wrong.

He heard a rustling and then a crash behind him, spinning around he could see where a tree had seemingly fallen onto the path behind him. The green, wire fence had splintered open and the securing pins that were put into the concrete pillar had pinged out. He poked his face further toward the concrete pillar. It had something written on it, cast into the concrete, almost indiscernible.

His concentration was cut short by the appearance of a colossus now arising beside him. The tree that had fallen was now getting up.

One huge, powerful goat like hoof planted itself on the dusty chalk behind him, then another, then finally a third as the thing rose up to it full height. It must have been at least twenty feet tall. What seemed to be branches now revealed themselves to be tentacles, masses of them slapping and flailing revealing gaping, fanged mouths that dripped an effervescent ichor that was appalling to the nose. Aside the mouths, seemingly at random there were spaced the occasional lidless eye, staring, coldly staring.

As Stayves came awake with a start he was not sure whether he had screamed out in the dream or in real life on the sofa.

The sounds of the passing cars on the road seemed wholly at odds with that purple toned horror, its maws open to meet him.

He picked the now empty glass of whisky off his lap. "Aww, bloody hell", he had thrown the spirit over his shirt and trousers. He'd have to find clean clothes for the morning.

His watch was reading 2.25AM. There was no way he was going to get back to sleep after whatever that phantasm was, the best idea would be a long bath and a big breakfast.

Maybe even turn up early at the station for once? Despite his best efforts it was hard to turn his attention away from that nightmare.

So, here he was, back again. Five thirty in the morning, fully fed, clean (but crumpled) clothes but feeling exhausted. He'd let himself in to the building via the back door by the mini car pool. He still hadn't worked out the main door with all its modern alarms and locks. He didn't fancy the local press taking pictures of him trying to get into the station whilst all the alarms and flashing lights were going on.

After a short bout of banter with the cleaner, who called him 'Hefe' and had blagged him for half a dozen cigarettes, he sat down at his desk with a cup of instant coffee and a couple of biscuits that had been left in the office biscuit barrel.

After that dream the place seemed oddly cold and quiet. He must be getting the jitters, it was almost like someone was watching him.

He turned on his rickety dining chair to open the blinds a fraction and look outside. The car park was quiet, the only thing he could see was a dark van, parked on the road opposite, with what appeared to be someone inside smoking a cigarette, the occasional glow of amber illuminated the interior of the cab against the overcast and rainy late summer morning.

Must be someone waiting for a workmate? Maybe he's some plumber or spark who's just having a crafty fag before his mate gets into the van?

There was an almighty bang on his desk.

Stayves jumped, sending a fair portion of his coffee spilling over his knees and wincing in shock as he spun around in the chair.

"Faecal matter"!

Marks was there. The forensics man had dumped a small stack of papers and photos on his desk and was pointing at the stack of four biscuits balanced on his memo pad.

"What the hell are you playing at? I could've crapped my pants". Stayves grabbed a spare set of socks he kept in his drawer and began stabbing at the spilled coffee to mop it up.

"Faecal matter on the biscuits. You got them out of the barrel. Everyone knows that publicly accessible foodstuffs like that are covered in excreta and are crawling with bacteria". He pushed his glasses back up his nose.

Stayves looked at the small stele of biscuits, they were covered in chocolate too. He lifted the memo pad, wrapped the biscuits in a fold of paper and stuffed them in his jacket pocket. Next door's cat could have them later. His socks went back in the drawer.

"Can I help you or are you just here for a friendly visit"?

"I managed to get the blood tests done overnight, I've been up all night too developing these photographs.

You've got to see them inspector". His hands were shaking as he opened the brown card file to begin presenting the contents.

"The bloods, that was fairly straight forward. Type O, human, initially we thought the traces were only on the stele, the rest animal; but no, they appear to issue from the main area of blood about eight feet away on some bizarrely flattened grass. This area was heavily contaminated with the same blood, likely pints of it. Suggesting the bloodletting of one or more people all of the same blood group".

"So you mean one person then"? Stayves swigged at his coffee, wrinkling his nose at the taste.

"More than likely".

"Some sort of freakish sacrifice considering the stele then"?

"You're the detective, detective Inspector; but I think that would be a reasonable supposition".

Marks put both hands on the desk now, his tie was hovering over Stayves' rolodex as if it was about to get trapped in it.

"It's the photos that are really interesting though. Here, look at this", Marks handed him a group of photographs, all black and white, eight by twelves that still smelt of processing.

He looked at the first, a square object had rutted the ground and flattened the grass; it must have been heavy. A clue to its shape was given by the large patches and sprays of blood that covered the ground around it.

How had he missed all that?

The next couple were of similar patches of blood with accompanying rulers on the floor and annotations of

the distance and geographical location from the stele.
The blood was sprayed over the clearing in patches.
"These ones are the real turd on your teacake".
Stayves winced at the forensic investigator.
The photos showed a grainy shot of what looked like a
hoof print, a cloven hoof print.
"Sheep"? He looked up at Marks.
"No, *Capra aegagrus hircus,* East European domestic
goat. Have a look at the ruler next to the print though".
Stayves looked down and tossed the papers on his
desk, his face ashen.
Marks nodded at the top photo.
"Those hooves measure over eighteen inches across".

Chapter 4

Stayves had spent a few moments turned away from
Marks, who was poring over the photographs and
mumbling to himself.
Was that dream he had had of that hideous thing with
the hooves some sort of hunch? Had he seen the prints
on the ground and not even realised it?
"Okay Sherlock, what else can we get from this lot"?
He slurped at his mug of tepid coffee and winced again
at the cheap chicory after taste. "That hoof print looks
deep, very deep. That was one hefty goat". He nodded
at the uppermost photograph.
"Yep, and probably tall too, notice how the print is flat,
there's no part of the hoof that hits the ground and digs
in first", the forensic scientist tapped at the photo and
then retrieved a close up of the stele's base.
"It's hard to see but you can just make out the ring
where the grass has regrown after the stele has been
erected here. Given the time of year I'd hazard a guess
that the monolith has only been there for a few weeks
based on that grass growth".
"Maybe the hefty goat ate all the grass"? Stayves tilted
his head sarcastically.
"Well, the fact that there is no traces of lichens like
Xanthoria parietina suggests that the stele is only a few
weeks out in the sun too".
"So, it could be essentially brand new"?
"Or it's been stored undercover for a while. That mix of

bank-run gravel with the concrete doesn't go much further back than the turn of the century. Plus, the twisted steel that supports it inside couldn't predate the war. Not for an extravagance like that".

"Twisted steel inserts? You mean like a fence post in a garden or something"?

"Yep, the very same. Anyway, I've used up enough of your time. We've only got the rest of the morning with the stone before it goes to evidence so I better get over and keep at it".

"Yeah, cheers Marks." Stayves neatened the folder and placed it in his sock drawer.

"Oh, and Marks?" the forensic scientist turned and halted.

"Bloody good work at short notice".

Marks grinned his toothy grin.

"Nice that someone appreciates it". He left the office, failing to close the door as he did so.

Stayves turned back to his coffee and stared out of the window blankly, maybe it was the lack of sleep, maybe not, but this whole escapade was beginning to get out of hand. It had to be some sort of ruse or prank.

Yet, that dream? It was almost as if someone were trying to tell him something?

"Mornin' Guv", Davies' chirpy accent cut across the morning silence.

"Bloody Nora, you too"? Stayves turned on his seat downing the last of his brew.

"Did you see your mate in the corridor"? Stayves asked.

"Who"? Davies looked blankly.

"Marks, the forensic fella".

"Oh, I don't know Guv, I'm still half asleep to be

honest".
"Nothing new there then"
"Eh"?
"I said you could do with a brew then. Get the kettle on and then tell me how you got on yesterday. It can't any weirder than the gubbins I've had this morning already".
"Right Guv".
Davies set the hot mugs of tea down on the desk and sat on the corner.
"I went around virtually everywhere I could think yesterday. Chandlers, building yards, that building site up near yours, even the council parks department; had a long chat with Chalky White there"…
"Chalky White"? Stayves interjected.
"Yeah, you remember him, he runs the local parks and gardens. We interviewed him over all the flowers getting nicked from roundabouts last summer".
"Oh, aye. How could we forget that caper"?
"Well, he was saying that they buy the readymade posts in from some place in Shropshire. Most places wouldn't even have the facilities to make a stone like the one we saw".
"Well that sounds like a dead end". Stayves paused for a moment, recalling his dream from the night before. Chalk pathway, he clearly remembered being on a chalk pathway and the fence that the creature burst through looked exactly like a council provided fence.
"Get a car ready for nine o'clock Davies. We may have to pay a visit to this Mr White guy again".

Chapter 5

He wasn't the type of bloke that believed in signs, mumbo jumbo or other juju superstition; he'd seen far too much of what happens at the rump end of humanity (and heard far too many tales of the excesses of the snout end in the trough). That said he had an almost ironclad feeling about the link between his dream and the name Davies had given him.

"So, why are we asking questions of this White fella again then guv? I thought I got everything out of him yesterday"? Davies asked.

"Just a hunch Davies, just a hunch".

Davies frowned and then pulled into the car park to the council's works department.

Stayves had spotted something as soon as they had rounded the corner. A parked car, a well maintained, blue Vauxhall Chevette was parked on the road outside. Yet this time its sides were sprayed with mud and divots of grass were visible beneath the wheel arches.

"Smethwick, that's bloody Smethwick's car", Stayves pointed at the blue Chevette.

"Nah, Guv, it can't be. He works at that big tyre place in town".

"Hero Tyres, Hero Tyres my arse. Let's have a butcher's at this shall we"? Stayves burst from the car in a fit of indignant mien. He left striding across the carpark, readjusting his overly tight jacket as he hurried toward the car.

It only took 30 seconds or so to identify the car, commit the mud and detritus on the car to memory. The discovery of cement dust on the back bumper and scratches on the paintwork where something heavy but thin had been placed protruding from the boot, evidently sitting on the folded down rear seats, told a story of its own.

The sight that caused him the most consternation though was the partially visible child's school satchel in the passenger footwell. His mind went back to the bloodstained grass clumps he had seen yesterday morning in that clearing and his face snarled at the thought of what this sod had planned.

He looked over at the large sheds of the works area and the many men who were sat outside in the overcast glow of the morning, some smoking, some chatting and drinking tea. He was not going to get anywhere trying to force an answer out of Smethwick, that much was certain. There had to be another way to sort this problem out and fast. Someone's life may depend on it. He bundled himself back into the Cortina, lit a cigarette, took a large draw and let the smoke out as he spoke;

"Smethwick's house, now".

Davies had complained solidly at the prospect of breaking and entering into Smethwick's house. He was intelligent enough to realise why his Inspector wanted to get to the residence while Smethwick was absent.

"We're saving up for a house Guv. I can't afford to get the sack. I've got a wife and kid to feed as well. It's okay for you in your flat".

"You can sit outside and listen to your pop songs on

the stereo constable. I'll do all the dirty work. If you see this bloody lunatic coming just beep your horn and try to stall him".
As the car pulled in to the cul-de-sac the place was quiet. Not only was there no sound of birds or beasts but also a lack of people. No swarthy, headscarved crones to pry and spy on his actions.
"I won't be five minutes, any aggro beep that horn", Stayves threw his lighter and cigarettes onto the dashboard and rifled inside the glove box, eventually retrieving a small case of lockpicks from the back of the compartment.
"Bloody hell Guv. Don't do this. You're in enough crap already". Davies stopped as the car door closed shut. Stayves reached the back gate, picking the lock on the front door was just too obvious. He tried the latch and breathed a slow sigh of relief as the gate opened. He was a little too rotund now for climbing over back walls.
As he entered the back garden area he could see a shed in front of him and the back door to the house on his left. The shed might hold something interesting but it was more important that he check the house first. Maybe his intuition again, maybe not.
He opened the pick case and drew out a slim tension tool and inserted it into the lock. It was quickly followed by a wire-like hook pick which he used to push and press at the pins as he kept the case dangling, gripped between his teeth.
It seemed like days had passed before the familiar click of the last pin and the turn on the tension tool told him the lock had succumbed.
He gulped down the trepidation, stuffed the picks into

his jacket pocket and went inside.

An ordinary kitchen, nothing to worry about. He felt the kettle, it was cold, and so was the hot tap. He moved on to the hall, he would forego the living room, he'd seen that already; it could wait till he'd had a good look around.

The dog. The damned dog. He'd forgotten about it. The creature had been snoozing at the base of the front door and now looked at him with a gathering annoyance.

He raised his finger to his lips to quieten the dog. The dog ignored him and let out its first bark; its hackles rising and tail standing on end.

"Aw shit", he thought. Yet that gave him an idea. Stayves reached into his pocket and pulled out the paper wrapped biscuits. He just wish someone could have seen how well prepared he was for any eventuality.

Wasted talent.

He threw the biscuits down at the door mat as the dog yelped and set at them in hunger. Who knows when the poor thing had been fed last?

He decided that speed was the issue; a few digestives don't deter the dogged doggy, he thought to himself as he puffed his way up the stairs.

There was a muffled noise coming from one of the rooms, he was sure it was the bathroom. As he started toward the noise the dog began barking again.

There was no sound of the horn, the damned thing must have finished the biscuits.

Stayves pushed aside the door to the bathroom and heard a distinct thump, even above the racket the dog was making. It was coming from the attic trapdoor in the ceiling. A muffled scream could be heard now.

Placing his foot on the wooden towel box on the floor let him reach up high enough to snap back the bolt that was holding the trapdoor closed.

A small, dusty face emerged over the edge of the ledge. It was the face of a young boy, not even nine, his hair tangled with loft insulation and his eyes filled with tears of bewilderment and terror.

"Hop down son, I'm the Police. I'll catch you".

The boy's eyes flashed a moment of relief and then widened again in horror as he pointed past Stayves and into the landing.

"He's one".

Stayves turned to see Davies behind him, his hands fumbling near the bathroom sink.

"What the hell are you doing? You're supposed to be keeping watch"? Stayves raised his voice against the noise of the dog's barks.

Davies' eyes struck him immediately. They were as wide as the boy's but this time maddened, almost rolling.

"You pressed too hard' Guvna", he spat the word out now. "Now you learn the potency of Shub Niggurath and the power she gives her faithful".

Davies slashed at him with the opened cutthroat razor he had picked up from the sink.

Stayves stepped back away from the attack at his abdomen and knocked over a small tower of toilet rolls, moving aside as they fell to the cheap carpet.

The boy had dropped down now from the attic and had bolted. He heard the pounding on the stairs as the lad ran, even above the noise of the now apoplectic dog. Confusion reigned, it must be age.

The razor came back at him and he drew his left arm to

cover himself as it slashed at him, cutting through his elbow skin. He could feel it but it caused him no pain. It was dulled, almost as if it were merely a piece of ham he was holding out.

Davies caught his eyes again, this time his partner, ex-partner, was sneering and almost salivating with some kind of maddened bloodlust.

Davies lunged with the razor as Stayves shifted to the left. The lockpicks from his jacket pocket went cascading through the air as Davies' thrust went past him, merely tearing the lining in his suit.

Stayves had collected himself. As Davies tried to rise back up from his attack the Inspector let out a heavy blow with the outside of his fist, straight into Davies's jaw.

There was a vague click as his ex-partner, spun and then collapsed into the bath; supine, eyes still wide but now devoid of consciousness and tongue lolling.

He was still breathing at least. He'd have a hell of a lot of explaining to do when he came around.

Stayves' first priority was to find the boy. He set off down the stairs to find the front door wide open and the dog now barking at the outside and then spinning around to bark at him on the stairs.

"Shouldn't have given him those biscuits, the bloody thing's pumped full of energy now". He stomped down the last few stairs into the hallway and looked at the gathering throng on the lawn. None of them were faces he could recognise, they all had the same blank expression and the same dark, surreptitious stares. There must have been twenty or so at least, crowding about the doorway and looking in, eyes narrowing in an abnormal curiosity. The women wore headscarves,

the men sported black bushy, thick eyebrows and
sideburns.

The exit was blocked.

Stayves turned and ran back to the kitchen, the dog
pursuing him, still barking, more out of confusion than
annoyance now.

He threw open the back door and rushed to the back
gate. It was wide open. Davies must have left it that
way. That means the boy must have opened the front
door and fled.

He sprinted, well, jogged, toward the Granada as the
group of residents clamoured and shouted their jarring
jaunts into the house. The dog had stopped on the drive
and had reduced its output to only sporadic gruffs
now.

Stayves slumped down on the driver's seat with the
door still open; he grabbed at the radio handset.

"Bravo Hotel Seven, this is Alpha India Two Three,
over". The radio clicked as he let go of the transmitter.
He looked at the door of the house. They had heard
him and were now moving toward him.

"Davies, have you dealt with him? Have you dealt with
him"? The voice was urgent, on the correct frequency
but had given up all radio protocol.

He threw down the radio handset in disgust and
started the car just as the mob enveloped the Granada.
Shoving the thing into gear he roared away across a
lawn, back tyres spinning on the thin grass as a couple
of the residents slid off his bonnet. One had managed
to grab the open door and was holding on to the
steering wheel attempting to pull the car into the wall
of a nearby house. Stayves managed to wrench the
wheel back the other way so that the door, and the

resident, smashed into a sturdy birch tree. Both the door and the resident disappeared as he sped away out of the cul-de-sac.

"Davies, are you there? Have you sorted him out"?

He looked down at the radio again, winced at the blood spraying from his elbow and then turned the volume control off.

"What the hell do I do now"?

Chapter 6

Stayves pulled the al-fresco Granada over into a pub car park. He could murder a pint but the car, his nerves, the bloodied suit and the fact that he was seemingly being hunted by the local force made him opt on the side of caution.
Plus, it was only twenty past eleven. They weren't even open yet.
He fumbled for a cigarette out of the gold packet and used his fist to shove the filter into his dry mouth. After three attempts with his zippo he eventually got the thing lit, drawing heavy breaths of smoke as he calmed down.
He kept the cigarette in his mouth as he tugged at his jacket gingerly to remove it. The lining of the sleeve was caked in blood, as was his shirt. Trying to peel back the shirt sleeve revealed that the wound was already coagulating and sticking to the shirt. He shrugged, that had to be a good thing, and rolled both sleeves of the shirt up.
He tossed the dying cigarette from the open doorway and lit another.
A two fag problem.
He couldn't go back to the station; that much was obvious. He couldn't use the radio. He only had notes, so no 2p pieces for the 'phone. Going into a shop for change might arouse suspicion.
He snorted, he'd spent so long around criminals that

when the time came to be a fugitive himself he didn't have a bloody clue. He had neither the funds nor the friends to feel safe at the moment.

"I'll go back to my flat. That's the obvious thing. Get some clothes and stuff, get somewhere else and sort this out from there. They'll never believe I'd go somewhere as obvious as that".

He tooled the Granada out of the pub car park and stayed away from the main roads, sticking to the back roads where he knew the local panda cars wouldn't patrol.

He eventually came to a no through road next to the park, one street away from his flat. A group of kids stopped their game of football and looked at the doorless Granada with a mix of shock and mirth. Stayves emerged, greying hair dishevelled, eyes, cheeks and nose ruddied from exertion and looked at them.

"Mind the car will you lads", he tossed the keys onto the driver's seat.

"Bit late for that mister", replied the cocky one with the freckles.

Stayves shook his head and walked up the cobbled alley between the two streets.

"Bloody cheeky sods".

That kid from the attic must have made it out okay. He definitely went down the stairs, Stayves had heard him. He would've seen the dog and moved away, back into the kitchen and the open back door and gate just as Stayves had done.

The living room

He hadn't checked the living room. The kid might have fled in there to hide. He stopped and bared his teeth in anger at himself.

"Why the hell didn't I check the living room"?
He stopped again at the end of the alley to peer around
the side of a badly maintained privet bush to look over
at his flat. It seemed quiet. His eyes though were drawn
to a familiar parked black van which was across the
road from his flat's entrance. That same black van
again.
He had just carefully returned a piece of privet back to
its place when two short toots on a car horn burst out a
jaunty welcome behind him.
Stayves turned slowly in trepidation.
A small, green Austin Allegro was parked in front of
him. It contained a long man in a green packamac who
was giving him the thumbs up sign and baring a very
toothy grin.
"You've got to be bloody kidding me"? Stayves hurried
toward Marks' car, getting in quickly without looking
at the black van.
"What the hell are you doing here"? Stayves was
genuinely shocked.
"I could ask the same. You are still on your shift and
you appear to be sneaking off home, it's not even
midday yet".
"Just get me out of here for God's sake". Stayves
grabbed a copy of "Melody Maker" from the
dashboard and buried his head in it as the little allegro
sped past the van.
"I am assuming by your testy behaviour and
bloodstained arm you are in some sort of trouble"?
Marks turned left onto the high street and in a moment
they were away from the van and the watching eyes
within.
"I've had a bit of a morning, let's put it that way. You

wouldn't have anywhere where I could doss for an hour or two, just to get my bearings"?

"As it happens, I was on my way home when I popped in to see you, saw the state of your desk in the office and then called over for you. I thought you'd wrecked your desk and resigned or something. I found you weren't in and was here finishing my tuna sarnie when you appeared".

"What's up with my desk"?

"Well, given that you obviously don't know anything about it I assume someone has rifled through your desk and taken all those photos and reports I gave you this morning. Possibly, something to do with that black van that was outside your flat? The same black van that was outside the window when I saw you earlier".

"You should've been a detective Marks".

"Call me Trevor". Marks said.

"Call me Stayves", replied Stayves. "Anyone ever told you, you drive like a vicar"?

"I drive carefully Inspector. You're the law, you should appreciate that".

"So *you* read the Melody maker then"? Stayves put the magazine down on the dashboard.

"No, that's Tom's, my nephew. He's staying over at mine for the weekend while his Mum and Dad have a break from him, they only live in Southport".

Chapter 7

Marks' flat was meticulous; pretty much as Stayves had expected. Open plan, one bedroom, seemingly no girlfriend, but lots of books, lots and lots of books.

His host went straight for the fridge as they arrived, removing two cans of beer; their dark green cans glistening near frozen moisture and a tinfoil tray that had once been used as an ashtray.

"Take a seat inspector, you could do with a drink", He proffered a space on the settee and placed the ashtray and a can down on the coffee table, opening his own can with a hiss of gas as the ring-pull was removed and discarded to a nearby bin.

Stayves leaned back into the couch and opened his own can, spilling beer onto his shirt which he dabbed at with his wide woollen tie.

"Tom", Marks nudged his nephew who was sitting on the other side of the room with a pair of headphones on. The long spiralled cord of which was plugged into an impressive looking record player and tape deck. The loud rock music was clearly audible even from the distance Stayves was sitting. The kid just ignored his uncle and carried on reading the album cover he was looking at.

"Tom", Marks nudged him again, this time harder. The kid tore off his headphones and turned, petulantly, his nose creased up in contempt and his curly brown hair hanging over his eyes.

"Tom, this is Inspector Stayves. I thought you might like to say hello". Marks led Tom's gaze to where Stayves was sitting on the settee doing damage to his can of beer.

"Right son, you listening to that Pink Purple music"? Stayves knew exactly what the kid was listening to, he'd heard it on pub juke boxes quite a bit but it payed to have a studied indifference to what current youth trends were all about.

"My name's Tom, Tom Earley, which is kind of funny 'cos I rarely am." The kid put the headphones back on and looked back at his album cover. He must have only been about ten years of age. Youth was not improving as the generations progressed.

"Nice little bugger isn't he? Don't know where he came from but do they do refunds"? Stayves lit up a cigarette.

"Yes, he is a little, erm, strongwilled", Marks looked at his nephew and shook his head.

"Kid will probably grow up to be either a serial killer or a right pain in the arse", thought Stayves, as he flicked ash into the can in front of him. Noticing his error, he shook the can to distribute the contents with the ash and replaced it with Marks' can. He needed this to steady his nerves.

He stubbed out his cigarette into the tinfoil tray and looked out of the window glugging at the almost full can of beer he had purloined.

"I'm going to have to borrow your car for a bit later on if that's okay"?

"Oh no, you're not going anywhere in that car without me driving it. My car won't survive your James Hunt antics", Marks sipped at his beer and winced.

"Bad pint"? Stayves betrayed a thin grin.

"Seems distasteful cans are the order of the day", he gestured at Tom's headphones and then put the beer down on the table.

"Right, this is what I was thinking for a way of proceeding with this investigation", Stayves looked over at Marks as he emerged from his bedroom with a haversack and his packamac rolled up into a small pouch.

"Ready when you are".

Stayves closed his eyes and pinched the top of his nose; it was never like this on the cop shows on the

television.
Chapter 8
"Does he have to come"? Stayves pointed to Tom in the back seat. The kid frowned back at him silently.
"He's been in all day inspector, we're only going for a look around. I thought a bit of mental stimulus might do him good".
The car pulled out from the street outside Marks' flat. The indicator's clicking seemed overly loud in the tense atmosphere inside the little allegro.
"Not so much a stake out as a bloody Sunday school outing. I'm surprised you didn't bring a bloody picnic". The car returned to silence for a moment as Marks maintained a sensible speed to the destination.
"Are you sure the council depot is open on a Saturday"? He turned to Stayves with a quizzical side glance.
"It was open this morning. If it's not we'll go to his house"
"Oh yeah, and have half the estate down on us after your debacle this morning"?
"Trevor, I'm in a lot of crap right? Do us a favour and just leave out the griping until we find out what's going on eh"? Stayves did his best frown and shook his head. The little allegro pulled up slowly outside the council depot, the bustle of earlier had subsided but White's car was still there, only this time in a different parking space.
"Right, park up here and we'll just wait until our little friend comes to collect his car. I really do wonder where you'll be going old Chalky boy", Stayves nustled deep into the chair to get comfortable.
"Should've brought more tea and butties", Marks

rummaged in his haversack and retrieved a small repast of hot tea and sandwiches.

"Nice one", Stayves was soon helping himself to the hot beverage and dunking his butty into the plastic cup of tea.

"You said that these people seem to be involved in black magic then?" The voice belonged to young Tom; his eyes had peered over the top of the Melody Maker he was reading.

"Yeah, I think so. They have a fondness for stelae and some sort of ritual magic; based on the forensic data we picked up. Why?" Asked Marks.

"Well it would seem that today is the 23rd of September, the feast of Mabon. One of the most important nights of the dark art's calendar". Tom said nonchalantly.

"How the hell do you know that"? Stayves turned to look at him.

"It's here in this write up on WytchForke, that new black metal band playing this weekend in London. Apparently this is a big time of the year for black magic so they're having a big gig tonight to celebrate". Tom retreated behind his Melody Maker.

"Sounds wholesome", Marks wondered aloud.

"Sounds bloody ominous to me". Stayves swigged at his tea and finished off the last of his soggy sandwich.

"It's just harvest home. The end of the traditional harvest time. We used to burn some of our crops or throw some mead and beer on the fields to say thank you. Now we take a few cans of soup to our local church or scout hut. Much more convenient". Marks said, absent-mindedly tapping his fingers on the wheel of the car.

It was an interminable hour or two. Both of the adults in the front were starting to cramp up in the small space in the front and the radio had been turned off due to constant bickering about the music (mainly from Tom, the back seat DJ).

"Eh up, here we go", Stayves raised in his seat and gestured toward three men leaving the yard. All carrying small backpacks. One was definitely 'Chalky' White.

"I don't see Davies there", said Staines.

"Hopefully he's still sparked out in the bath", Stayves frowned again.

"Get the car started, we're not going to lose him". Marks packed the thermos and empty sandwich foil into his haversack, threw it onto the backseat and started the car.

Chalky White's car reversed, turned and then cruised past them. The driver turned for a moment and ran his eyes past Marks but flashed no form of recognition. Marks turned his own vehicle and moved off after them. Stayves guffawed to himself at the speed of both of the cars. They both must be doing twenty miles an hour each. It was akin to a road race for reverends. White's car moved across the suburban streets surrounding the council's parks and gardens yard and headed out into the open farm fields and narrow lanes of the agriculture area that sat behind the town where Marks resided. Though criss-crossed by narrow lanes which connected the various towns in the locality the roads were seldom used at this time on a Saturday night. Most people would be getting ready to go out or settling in for a night at home.

Most people.

The car moved along a series of lanes, still slower than necessary, until it drove up into an open gateway and onto a large field of maize. Marks followed Stayves' instructions and carried on driving, turning up into a similar opening between hedgerows only a few hundred yards up the lane.

"Looks like it's shank's pony from here", Marks said.

"Aye", replied Stayves.

"What are you two on about"? Tom wrinkled his nose and shook his head.

"You better stay here sunshine. Actually, no, come with us so we can keep an eye on you". Stayves looked at his colleague for approval. Marks nodded.

"And grab that haversack while you're at it". Marks nodded at the back seat as Tom grabbed the bag, slung it over his shoulder and followed his uncle, wrestling his way over the folded down driver's seat to exit the car.

It was gone six o'clock now. The September's warm air had turned cooler and the fading light would be struggling to reach seven o'clock in the evening. The red, autumnal moon was heavy in the sky. Only just peering above the top of the six feet maize plants that grew in the field.

Marks placed his foot on the car's front wheel before him and stood up to survey the field in front of him. It was lucky he was so tall, as the top of the familiar stele was only just visible across the corn, a few hundred feet away.

"Looks like your friend the stele's back". Marks said as he dropped down from the car tyre perch.

"I'm going to take a look. You two stay by the car". Stayves slid off his jacket to reveal the blood matted sleeve of his shirt.

"I want to see what's going on here, thank you very much", Marks reached over to Tom's shoulder and rummaged in the haversack. Soon retrieving a small but well maintained revolver from the bag.

"Where the hell did you get that"? The inspector looked aghast.

"It's my old man's service revolver. He had it in the war, never gave it back. It's fully loaded. Look" Marks snapped open the mechanism and bared the fully loaded revolver at Stayves before closing it with a sharp click.

"I'd better have that before you do someone a bloody mischief. I am the law".

"I am the law", laughed Tom.

Marks handed the gun over with a shrug.

Stayves looked down at Tom and frowned again.

Tom stopped laughing.

The trio set off into the high corn at a slow rate, surreptitiously trying to move the corn aside rather than break it. Both in an attempt to be quiet and also to make little or no motion on the top of the maize crop. The dull, red glare of the setting sun made an easy guide to where they were headed.

It was when they had reached the circle of crushed corn that they saw the stele; standing tall in the centre of a large area of maize that had been flattened in a concentric manner. White and his two colleagues had busied themselves preparing their robes, two of them in hooded robes of greens and browns and the swarthier of White's compatriots in a dark purple robe with a brown, oblong over garment.

Each had placed on a mask, White and his friend

donned what appeared to be woven faces made from vine leaves, only dark hollows of the eyes devoid of foliage. The purple clad man had pulled on an obscene, twisted, leering face, atop of which sat a multitude of brown, wound cloth tendrils which shivered and danced crudely as he moved his head. Each tendril was adorned with painted eyes and slobbering mouths. Stayves batted his palm down toward the floor as an order for them to kneel and take cover. Fortunately both Marks and Tom complied.

The blood moon was clearly visible above the flattened area, hanging low across the stele as if it were some hovering red bird awaiting its feast.

A nearby sound of engines and the sound of tyres on grass made the three men in the robes turn and view the area to the road. The sound of van doors slamming and muffled voices signalled that the other celebrants had arrived. The bleating of a pair of goats made the two adults look at each other in incredulity.

For Tom it was perfectly reasonable. Devil worshippers always had a goat or two lying around.

The new arrivals emerged from the narrow path that had been created through the maize. It was obvious that they had parked the vans down near the gate behind the high bushes and trees that made the hedgerow. There were about thirty of them, some in various states of robing, some wearing the same vine leaf masks, others carried them in their hands to reveal a mixture of skin tones from dark brown to pale white. Stayves had spotted two members of the local police and at least one member of the local council among the throng.

Noticeable amongst them were the two goats led on

ropes and a tall figure bound almost wholly in vine leaves, his bare legs sticking out of the coverings as if he were in some perverse sack race. The figure tramped, confusedly and was tugged at by the celebrants who were holding the ends of the ropes that were tied about its neck and waist. The leaves of its grapevine garment dripped a steady drop of liquid as though the figure had been saturated before entering the clearing. There was a distinct smell of alcohol; maybe brandy or whisky.

The man in the purple robes, gesticulated toward the stele causing the appendages on the top of his mask to cavort on his head obscenely.

The ivy man, for it was obviously a man, was tied to the stele with the ropes and joined by the two goats who were similarly tethered.

"Sacrifices", Marks whispered.

"Why the hell have they covered that bloke in plants"? Stayves asked in a low voice.

"If I recall my Robert Graves correctly, in 'The White Goddess' and his other book, he talks about there being certain trees associated with each month. I'm guessing that grapevine is the tree for September. It'd certainly make sense considering the smell of brandy and the harvest connection". Marks muttered indifferently. Stayves shook his head at this man's command of seemingly bizarre knowledge. He took the pistol from his belt and kept it in his right hand tightly.

"Just in case".

"I knew I should've asked Bette from reception out on a date", Marks mumbled to himself.

The nearest of the worshippers turned toward their hiding place, eyes hidden behind the mask of twisted

vine leaves. She peered at the maize for a moment and then turned back as the chanting started.
"Ia, ia, Shoob-Niggurat!
Black Goat of the Woods...of One Thousand Young!
Come forth by night...
Blessed be us; your faithful servants, oh eraser of the light!"
The purple robed priest intoned the words in a barely understandable, guttural voice.
"Ia, Ia!" chanted back the throng. Cowled heads bowed at the priest at the stele.
The celebrant drew a small steel and striker. With each strike and spark the bound man twitched and strained at the ropes.
On the third strike the alcohol soaked vines erupted in flames, drawing a breath from the crowd, a sickening, piercing screech from the terrified goats and a panicked and painful writhing by the bound and immolating victim.
"Ia Shoob-Niggurat"!! The priest raised his hands.
His followers followed his action, each raising their hands and bellowing.
"Ia, Ia, Ia"!
The cacophony was horrifying. Marks turned to a wide eyed Tom and shooed him away, back toward the car.
No child should see this.
For once Tom complied.
On a gesture from the priest the two nearest celebrants came forth and, wrestling an animal each let the spraying blood of the caprines across the partially charred man. The jets washing away the burnt stems of the vines, dropping to the floor in cremated, coagulating clumps.

"Davies, that's Davies".
Stayves narrowed his eyes, Marks was right, it was
Davies. Now a burnt and barely conscious shell of a
victim rope tied to a stone stele. That kid in the attic
must have escaped, he'd made sure his perfidious
partner had replaced him in that abominable fate.
The glutting had abated and the still of the now near
dark clearing descended. Yet again that eerie silence, no
cars, no birdsong, only the spasmodic twitching of
dying animals amidst the crushed corn.
A caw and a short beat of wings from a nearby group
of crows shocked the silence.
"Crows. The Morrigan, the Morrigan approaches",
Marks was ashen, mouth agape.
"The what"? Staynes had spoken out loud but no one
even flinched as he effectively gave their cover away.
A singular rasp. Booming in its baritone and then rising
sharply to a terrifying screech and then followed by a
series of hollow knocks that sounded like wood blocks
erupted from the maize opposite.
An ungulate abomination, taller than the tops of the
corn stems and wider than the three worshippers that
stood before it stamped one of its three hooves and
lashed and whipped its many tentacled top half as the
jaws and eyes on each tentacle snatched and leered
insanely.
"Oh, for the love of God", Stayves dropped the
revolver to the floor and looked in dumbed horror at
the thing. It was the exact same creature from his
dream. Now bathed in a sanguine glow from the blood
moon and the embers of the burning leaves and
charred maize at the base of the stele.
"Absolutely fascinating", mumbled Marks. He felt

around his immediate area for his haversack. He had to get the camera for a photograph. He could not see that Tom had taken it. He could not take his eyes from the mind shatteringly alien nature of the thing.

The creature erupted in another bellow, followed by that loathsome, wooden knocking noise. Presumably from some disgusting throat or hellish maw. As it finished it sent one of the cultists flying aside and slapped the other tentacles about the exsanguinated creatures and the now merely twitching, blackened man.

The creature tugged at what was left of Davies, the many mouths on the tentacles catching and biting his seared flesh as the stele gave way to the pressure and collapsed to the floor. He was pulled from it whole, like some obscene, skewered meat.

A second creature had come to join the feast. This thing was slightly smaller but just as loud. That clacking, cavernous disgrace of a noise sent chills down both listeners' chines.

Stayves' head had cleared slightly. He drew his eyes away from the horrors that fed on his former friend and looked down at the revolver.

"I am the law".

He drew the gun up and fired.

The resulting bang made everyone start. The bullet shot across the clearing pounding straight into the stomach of the high priest, exploding his red and brown viscera over the purple and brown garb. The celebrant screamed and collapsed to the ground.

Everything seemed to stop for a second.

"Good shot", said Marks.

"I was aiming for one of those things", Stayves replied.

Cocking the catch for another shot.

The creatures had located them. Both thundered forward, obstructed by panicking cultists who were trampled or batted aside by hooves or slapping appendages, leaving crushed or wrecked bodies in their wake.

"I think we better go", Marks put a hand on his friend's shoulder.

Stayves let off another shot. This time it found its mark. The slug burying itself deep in the bark-like skin of the beast. The thing let out an enraged roar as it pelted toward them at an alarming rate.

Marks began to back up in haste, grabbing Stayves' shirt he pulled at the inspector to get him to follow his retreat from the edge of the clearing. He had pulled his friend for ten feet, Stayves barely keeping his footing, when the smaller of the creatures was almost on them. Marks felt his hand wrenched free of the shirt as his comrade ripped his grip away. As Stayves let off another jarring blast from the pistol he screamed at the forensic scientist;

"Run Trevor. I'm not fast enough. Run and make sure"…

The tentacles of the thing lashed at Stayves and rent his chest asunder. With a scream and a wildly misaimed gunshot he fell to the ground beneath first one hoof, then a mass of feeding, flaying feelers.

"Oh shit, Ardwood, you bloody idiot". Marks fled as fast he could go. The larger creature was pursuing him now. It was visible by the ears and shoots of corn that erupted into the air as it thrashed. Croaking and rattling as it came.

His heart was racing, chest stabbing at him as he burst

his way through the stout staves of corn he had to bat aside.

Tom, he had to find Tom.

For every turn he made to see what was behind him he screamed louder as the thing gained on him. The corn wall seemed to be almost impenetrable as he forced at it to allow his passage.

Thinking he had been beaten and he had been running in circles, almost at his last breath and near sobbing at the thought of his failure he burst out onto the track at the edge of the cornfield.

Marks collapsed onto the floor and rolled over. Ahead, on the track, he could clearly see the lights and steaming exhaust of his little Allegro. The petrol fumes making a thick mist against the red haze of the rear lights.

He turned to view his assailant. The thing had almost joined him. He could see its own steam rising from its maws and the heated ichor and coted blood on its body. It made its own haze across the bloodied, crimson moon.

He raised himself and sprinted with whatever he had left. Battering into a worshipper who burst out of the corn and sending them spinning back into the crop. The thing had emerged onto the track. He could see it now, its many tentacles' eyes scouring for him in the poor light.

He was framed against the rear lights of the car, the creature drew itself round to face him. He had one last chance.

Marks launched at the car door and threw it open, bundling his gangly limbs into the cramped space under the steering wheel. He turned to see Tom looking with increasing horror into the passenger side mirror on the sun visor.

He turned to view through the back windscreen, hand brake off, foot on the brake. The sanguine light illuminated the beast as it rent its fury across the back of the car; splintering the rear screen and collapsing the thin metal of the boot and rear bumper. It pounded first one hoof and then another across the back of the vehicle. Shuddering the passengers in the now oversized tin can.

Marks felt sick again.

Failure.

"Uncle Trev. Reverse, put it in reverse", Tom was shouting at him, shaking his arm.

Marks responded automatically, slamming the car into reverse gear, flooring the accelerator and then letting off the clutch.

The Allegro heaved and revved in protest and a searing wail came from behind the car.

The creature's leg that was still on the earth had been bent and flattened beneath the car. The tentacles flailing and battering at the now collapsed in rear window.

"Drive, go, go, go". Tom shouted, now hoarse.

Marks put the car into first as the Allegro limped down the path and away from the thing. Slamming it into second he hit the road the car sped away with a series of loud bumps, scrapes and rattles.

"Stayves"? Tom asked dolefully.

Marks shook his head and stared at the road ahead, no longer ashen. Now bleached bone white.

Tom followed his stare.

"Where are we going Uncle Trev"? Tom clutched tightly at the haversack, now his own.

"We're going to your Mum and Dad's; we're going for a very, very extended stay at your Mum and Dad's".

Ravers

It was the alarm that woke me. It was a screeching tone at first but then died in a matter of a moment to nothing, as if someone had yanked its plug out. I lay there silently, not moving, pillow soaked with sweat, the smell and taste of puke sitting over me like a damp flannel.

There was the brief scream of a woman and then the smashing of glass, something large, like a window. My eyelids toiled to open and present me with the glaring light of the room. The uncanny silence had returned at the same time my focus had. The mirror opposite me showed my pitiful face and drooped eyes staring back with the full regalia of the night before. This was a hotel room. That much was obvious, the décor was either a hotel room or a newly decorated house for rent. Only those places put towel bundles next to the bathroom sink which was visible from the bed. Plus, I wasn't in the habit of being violently ill in newly decorated upmarket houses for rent, at least I hadn't been so far.

I raised myself onto a bruised and cut elbow, relieved at the padding of the mattress, and scanned the room through blinking eyes. The spilled contents of my suitcase, the empty vodka bottle on the floor, the curtains blowing from the breeze through the open window.

I stretched my other arm back to pat the bed behind

me, just to check whether anyone was there. The bed was barren but for my bare body. It was with a considerable sense of uncertainty that I pushed my legs from the bed and righted myself, rubbing at my sore eyes with curled up hands.

I was on the island; now I began to recall. The dance capital of the world, invite only, for the great, the famous and, or, the beautiful.

Each generation, with toil and tears, has had had to earn their heritage again; but not ours. Ours was handed to us safe, with no bar code we could scan to gauge its worth. That's how we party.

My temporarily unreliable legs got me to the window for a heaving breath of hot, stale air. The place smelt of sweat, grime, alcohol and a few other olfactory experiences that I could not summon to memory at that moment.

A scream rang out from beyond the room's door again. This time ending in a loud shriek and a few muttered laughs. Something about the silence that buffered the sounds made my skin crawl.

Locating a tee shirt, shorts and a pair of flip flops was easy, there were enough spilled out of my suitcase that had opened out over the chair.

I returned to the sink and mirror to splash some chilled water over my face and hair, hoping the wet look might prevent anybody recognising me until I had figured out what had happened last night.

I could remember leaving the room. We had finished the vodka and were all laughing. Then we are near one of the dance floors and I was drinking something out a bottle. Then there was something wrong with the lights. After that a blank. A complete blank.

I rinsed my mouth with some of the complimentary mouthwash and spat the remains out in the sink. I think I had preferred the appalling taste before I had sampled the mouth cleanser.

As I opened the door and looked back at the room I was struck by the orange glow that was coming from the windows, both in my room and in the corridor outside. It almost seemed as if it was twilight. I looked at my smartwatch

1.25PM

The satsuma glow of the sun, combined with the uncanny silence of the hotel, made my skin crawl for the second time.

The corridors were wide, framed in gold leaf, hardwood and high quality painted plaster. Some walls were adorned with fine mosaics. Here and there on the crimson carpet runners there were scattered empty bottles, small zip lock bags, discarded tobacco and even a few syringes.

Maybe even the cleaners had a late one?

I made it to the end of the corridor, straightening up as I went, my muscles starting to realise that their effort was required. The view opened up into the large mezzanine that overlooked the main lobby. That strange orange sunlight bled into the place through the large, tinted windows which lent the whole area an unhealthy, jaundiced tinge.

A clatter below me made my eyes lower over the ledge of the wooden balcony and scour the tiled hall below me, here and there were abandoned clothes, bags, trays and other discarded paraphernalia from the night before. The signs of some serious abandon were abandoned all over the lobby.

My eyes were drawn to a group of people who were stooped over a body lying in the centre of the main entrance area, they were manhandling it as one of their number, a bald headed man in a sleeveless vest and shorts pointed up at me and maintained his gesture as his colleagues followed his prompt.

It seemed like some time had passed before they gave a shout and started running for the nearest stairs to gain the same level I was on.

I paused for a second and then dropped to the floor, running through the options in my mind. Had I interrupted some sort of altercation? Were these people local law enforcement officers or hotel security? They did not seem like any sort of official group.

My addled mind opted for a group of local thieves who were taking advantage of the lack of available staff on the premises. I considered it wise to make my way around the circular balcony and snake down the stairs on the opposite side to my adversaries.

It was with a new scream and a series of fresh calls and shouts, glass shattering and running feet that my pursuers peeled away from the edge of the balcony to chase down closer prey.

As I reached the foot of the stairs and headed for the exit a solitary scream rang out from the upstairs balcony, followed by pounding footsteps. I hastened from the hotel casting glances behind me as I went.

The sickened glow of the sun stopped me in my tracks as I emerged into the pool area. A huge, bilious ruined sun hung like a pensile, orange pustule in the firmament. The water, the white concrete pavers, even the tended plants in the various raised beds, all had a sickened orange hue. It was as if I had entered some medieval Limbo; a den of demons and the partially damned.

As I walked past the pool, moving in between the sun loungers, towels, glasses and bottles that littered the pool side. I noticed a small stall was set up near the end of the bathing area. I hurried toward it as the owner was still sat behind the stall looking out toward the coast.

My haste was proved unnecessary as my arrival at the stall was greeted by the grotesque site of the owner's dispatch being from savage wounds to his face. The sunglasses he wore masked gouged out eyes, now wholly viewable as I snatched off the dark, plastic spectacles. The blank, black holes in his face, where once his eyes had been, looked like parodies of dark glasses themselves. The blood stains that ran down his cheeks showed that his blood was flowing when this had been done to him; he was alive to endure the mutilation. He was not alive now, his open mouth that seemed like a yawn at a distance was stretched open in a silent scream.

At one of his wrists and at both of his ankles, his flesh had been secured to the chair with windings of tight wire that cut into his skin. It almost seemed to be a form of torture that had been carried out His body was positioned carefully, pointing out to the littoral landscape about half a mile away over a dry, barren rise. Around his neck hung his sign;

SHADE'S $20

Beneath the price someone had written the words, 'rip off'. I had to agree with them, though not with their means of showing it, even with the misplaced apostrophe.

I walked away from the abomination, darted my head around at any perceived movement in this now alien environment.
Were the people that did this the same people that were back in the hotel? It must be some sort of gang warfare. There was no other explanation.
I followed the bloodied hand of the sunglasses vendor toward the coast, taking the old, dusty road that was used by the locals to bring some of the produce to the resort. It was lined with dry stone walls and fast growing clumps of wild coriander which lent a sickly orange scent to match the sickly orange sky. A sky that looked wounded and tender like a fresh blow upon an old bruise.
I had been walking for a few minutes, still eager to evade anything that might be hiding in waiting or eager to set upon me, when I looked upon the field next to me. My attention was initially drawn by the oddly ebbing sound of white noise coming from the area. I had, at first, thought it the sound of the sea but as I drew closer if was obviously mechanical in nature.
The field itself was a morass of churning mass, was it moving in time to the ebb of that noise? I looked more closely and noticed that the moving mass was not that of mud or earth but the serpentine slithering of bodies, naked bodies, perhaps thirty or forty of them. They writhed in the churned up earth clawing and grasping at one another salaciously. Here and there bite marks dripped flesh blood into the ooze as faces emerged from the mass with vacant, yet insane, staring eyes, only to disappear into the brownish grey churning paste in which they cavorted.
My head was starting to spin as I entered the field and

came across an oddly incongruous looking coffee table
that sat next to the gate. On it was a set of speakers, and
MP3 player and a few knives. They were obviously
looted from a nearby shack or farmhouse.
The speakers were responsible for the white noise I was
hearing, yet now I was closer I could hear a vague
drone of voices within the distorted sound. The voices
were slowed down, almost indecipherable. Odd,
because the player had no moving parts, even if the
battery was dying there was no reason for the slowness
of the voice.
"Do it. Do it. Do it", the voice prompted, almost
inaudibly.
My mind was fuzzy, my sight had become blurry and
misty. It was all I could do to see my hand pick up the
knife as I staggered sideways into the field.
Do it… DO IT.
My eyes were wide now, I failed to blink to prevent the
spoiled sun from drying them out. As I lurched hither
and thither across the field edge they became sore and
stinging.
It was with a stagger and a slip that my footing was lost
in the churned earth, the knife was poised to strike as I
fell backwards, turning as I did so, to strike my jaw
across the dry rock of a fallen part of the dry stone wall.
I fell flat to the floor, unconscious.
I do not know how long I lay there. I remember
thinking I had endured a vivid nightmare, only to re-
emerge back into it when I opened my eyes. The
writhing field, the knife, the white noise; all still there
waiting for me.
I drew myself away on my hands and knees, through a
gap in the wall and stumbled away along the dry road,

retching at the smell of the field and the overbearing scent of coriander.

I had made my way some distance toward the beach area, now walking but still wary and monitoring the yellowed, dry fields on each side, separated from the road by those old dry stone walls. As I glanced at the stubbled soil to my right I saw a ripple moving along the earth toward me, almost as if there was a giant fish or other creature darting toward me under the earth. It presented no bow wave however, the entire ground was vibrating and shaking in a great wave that headed at me. Catching up with me as I grasped at the topmost loose rocks of the wall.

The earth bowed and waved below me, my stabilising grip on the wall leaving as the barrier collapsed into loose pieces. Ripple after ripple shook me onto my back and left me grabbing at the soil for something at least that might be solid and stable.

The entire tremor had gone as fast as it had appeared, a vague ringing sensation was left in my ears, more from the oscillation of my body in harmony with that of the earth than any noise that I had heard.

I rose to my feet and steadied myself once again against the dry stone wall. The majority of it had collapsed and fallen to the floor with the tremor that had passed by, some rocks falling onto the roadway and others into the field beyond. Dry cracks had formed on the surface of the compacted earth of the road, tiny canyons that split the steady compression of hundreds of years of busy toil by the villagers.

The village was in sight now, only a few hundred metres away as I stumbled along the ruptured road uncertainly. Its bright painted stucco walls, some salmon pink, others sky blue, seemed tinged by an unhealthy pallor from the tangerine sky. It was as if I was walking in the pages of a magazine, lens filtered pictures of some lost fishing village.

The place was empty, no signs of the industry I had expected from a once poor seaside corner to a gentrified purveyor of postcards and plastic gifts at steep prices. As I passed one small card shop I emerged into a small, cobbled square, the sudden smell of brine struck me as a small group of children stopped and turned to look at me.

There were five of them, three girls and two boys; the oldest must have been eight. They were dressed in beach finery, designer wear for those who care, yet they did not seem to be the children of any of the visitors to the place. Not many people who came to party on this island would bring children with them.

These seemed to be local children, their dark curly hair and olive complexions hinted at their aboriginal nature. I looked down at the cobbles to see what the object of their game was, maybe a ball or perhaps a box full of treats that they had found. I was taken aback by the face of an old woman, bloodied and bruised. Her hair was pulled, some of it missing clumps and her black dress was torn and hanging loose. Her upper arms had been beaten and already the rude bruises were beginning to show.

The children looked at me blankly, at first I thought I could read malice but then I realised that the blank stares were just that; pure mindless innocence. There was no hint of intention in their demeanour.

They turned to resume their assault, some with fists and feet, others with lumpen clubs made from firewood. As they lashed and struck the old lady shrieked and laughed maniacally, her eyes fixed on me as her head was rocked from side to side; her mad eyes glaring at mine, wide and unblinking.

It was folly to tarry. I set upon my course down to the coast without even glancing at the appalling act to my side, I was certain that the children did not even notice me as I hurried around the edge of a building and scurried along the cobbles toward the seashore. The screams and wails of the old lady convinced me that they were fully occupied.

As I left the village and headed past the many nets draped across the walls on the outskirts I finally found what had happened to the occupants of the resort and the village. The shoreline was a heaving mass of people. Some jumped and kicked at the waves in odd paroxysms, others stood swaying, mouths open and unblinking eyes staring at the sickened sun. Most were knelt, rocking back and forth muttering something incomprehensible, yet so familiar.

Ph'nglui mglw'nafh Cthulhu R'lyeh wgah'nagl fhtagn. Further out to sea, accompanied by the frantic screams of both adults and children there were groups of people, some had sliced at themselves to pour their life essence away as a sickened libation into the once crystal blue water. Others, presumably mothers from the village had led their children out into the deeper water and held their progeny before them for the circle sharks to pick off and feast. Their screams mixed with the wails of their former nurturers as the water splashed and sprayed with crimson foam.

A startling flash of light, brighter than the wearisome sun erupted across the sky, causing the heads of any

with any semblance of working senses to turn, there
were few.

The sight of the enormous mushroom cloud blooming
into the air to the North East left me somehow empty. I
failed to even respond as a few moments later the wind
battered at us and gave an odd phase to the screams
out to sea.

I cared little for the shuddering earth and sand below
me as I turned my eyes to follow the stares of my
fellow acolytes.

He was here, he had awoken. The race memories of the
human race erupted into my conscious mind. The
hidden knowledge that had been repressed by
millennia of silence and shuddering moments in
dreams. Yet he was greater in stature than any
nightmare had allowed, ore maddening in magnitude
than the greatest of night terrors.

I understood now the insane acts of my fellow
beholders. Who could live in a universe that could hold
such a monstrous behemoth, its pathetically small
wings, sat almost inconsequential on its back, flapped
ludicrously; a sneering slur on the need for flight. This
thing needed no speed to achieve its goal. Madness and
terror carried all before it.

I screamed as I saw its maw open beneath the mass of
glistening wet tentacles that hurried here and there
across its face like myriad elvers.

The ash descended as I waded out to sea to join the
bloodcurdling screams of the bloodstained and sprayed
throng. I too joined in the cacophony of a chorus for
Cthulhu. Waiting my turn for the sharks or the other
creatures with the tridents and the razor sharp, cruel
shell blades to deal with us.

I looked down to see a child's arm float at my waist, a plastic watch read 3.33. As I drew up my eyes, still screaming, the pain seared through me and I drew my last gasps, a sacrifice for this newcomer who was older than our race.

Town in the Moor

I never asked, nor did anyone ever tell me, why we went there. My mother said we should never look back. I assume it was because of my father's new position as the local policeman in charge of the small village of Moreton on the tip of the peninsula.
It was a small collection of houses, more cottages, that sat on oft flooded roads that led to a centre of sorts, of an inn and a few shops. To one side of this was the church of Christchurch, its rectory pulled down due to the influx of rot and mould recently and on the other side the road that led to the coast via the railway line. A road that was more used to rafts and rats than horses or vehicles. Alongside this road there were scattered groups of traveller camps tossed randomly across the ancient boggy fields. Buses, tents, old trams; the odd assortment of dwellings lined the road where the occupants would share the sodden grassland with the sandpipers and oyster catchers that clacked and screeched across the sea's edge.
We were never welcome in that place. I don't know whether it was because my father was a representative of the law in that lawless dive. The upper portions of the peninsular around Moreton had been a haven for criminals (and things far worse) for hundreds of years at least. The chronicler of Edward, the black prince had written, 'most gracious lord [the Black Prince] had taken into consideration the great harm, damage and hardships that the beasts of the forest of Wirral had

done continually to his common people there….' His men had attempted to level the entire area of sanctuary for beast and brigand alike. Even the Gawain poet had written in his fourteenth century poem *Sir Gawain and the green knight*, 'into the wilderness of Wirral, where there lived only few whom God or men of good heart loved'

A large lighthouse stood above the fields at the seafront with the fringes of the traveler camps reaching right up to it. This edifice was the oldest brick built lighthouse in the land (many said that it was so the local denizens could not burn it down as they had done the other one further up the coast). The lighthouse was said to have been laid upon a foundation of cotton bales that had been washed ashore from a shipwreck, a major source of income for locals at the time. No one ever mentioned why no sailor who survived the shipwrecks ever made it off the coastline alive though.

Each Sunday was a chore for my parents to prise me from the house to sit and sometimes kneel in that cold damp church. I can still remember the walk to the door and looking across the old graveyard to the tilled fields outside the fencing. Wishing I was anywhere but here on this invariably dark, foggy morning.

The Reverend R.L Gillswain would be waiting in his vestments; bulbous, unblinking wide eyes and that enormous, grimaced mouth; drooped at the ends and pulling at his fleshy, clammy visage to drag his eyes even wider open. His hand batted at the edges of his ill-kempt trousers to seemingly wipe away the clamminess of his palm before each handshake. As my father, who towered over him, and my mother, who could not abide him, moved past, his eyes would flash

with some perverse delight upon seeing me. That toad-
like tongue; bloated and black speckled, would lash
about at his cankered lips as his slimy hands ushered
me through the door.
His wife would play the organ for that tiny
congregation, the high collar of her blouse oddly
wheezing in and out as she played as if she breathed
through her neck rather than her nose. Her centre
parted hair pulled back so tight it too gave her a
maddened, wide eyed stare. Furrowed eyebrows and
deep bags beneath her eyes sat atop a chiselled thin
nose and a pursed grimace that had never even
grinned, never mind smiled. I always thought she
might be confused about what sort of creatures we
were as she glared and glowered, hunched over her
keyboard.
I made it a point to surreptitiously slip away after each
of those weekly services, ostensibly to get some air but
the atmosphere of that town was never conducive to
the lungs. The air was heavy and humid, its scent a mix
of salt and damp; damp wood and damp clothes, damp
people and damp faces.
I would make my way to the old millpond at the
eastern end of the town. An area of small ponds ringed
with hanging trees and long, unnaturally yellow grass.
I would sit by the ponds counting the seconds between
the loud pops of bubbles that would arise from the
black water. Whether it was marsh gas, some old,
wizened fish or something much more sinister, I never
really countenanced. All I know was that the place was
the closest I had found to a hiding place. Somewhere I
could sit and not feel like the scrutiny of those
townsfolk was upon me. A place where I could escape

the muffled whispers and narrowed stares that
accompanied my family wherever we went.
I was rarely alone near those ponds; it was a favourite
haunt of many of the travelers who would gather there
to drink their peculiar grog and sprawl across the alien
grass to hear the crying music of the gulls. To talk and
curse in their many accents; some I could understand
and some I could not with their chilling sounding
curses. Some of them looking like anyone you or I
might meet on any town in the country on an average
work-a-day afternoon. Others however had the same
look as the oldest residents of that town. The same
bulbous eyes and sickly, wet visage. Sometimes the
women would dance in a lewd and lascivious manner
as the men in the party guffawed and croaked; some
making loud gurgling and screeching noises as if they
were drowning.
It was on one such late morning that my recollection of
this singular series of events takes place. I had been sat
in my usual haunt. Aware only of the silence of the
place, even the wind seemed to hold its breath. The
same party of travellers approached the millponds
from the road that led to the coast; a short walk, and
were headed towards me at a drunken, laconic pace. I
can see them in my mind's eye; faded woollen
garments with tattered edges, old cotton here and
there, yellowed and badly cut.
They sat down beside the largest of the ponds, where
the trees grew from beneath the ankle deep, black
water. The trees grew as straight as staves and bore no
limbs until they were free of the gurgling air of that
sodden earth. Here and there were patches of that odd,
long yellow grass that sprouted like hairs on an old

paintbrush. They provided convenient seating points
for the revellers who were passing around flagons of
that clear brew that they drank. My mind fancied it was
a form of "moonshine" that the gangsters of the USA
would drink in the radio dramas I had listened to.
One of them played a small hand accordion which
wheezed out some form of jig, its cadence unsettling
and jarring. Another had fashioned a form of two note
pipe from a large shell which he used to intersperse
discordant notes, at random intervals, into the foul
sounding theme. The whole ensemble told me
something was wrong; that something was sickened
and askew with this group. The maddened, yellowed
eyes, the wide, leering mouths and the odd, awkward
jerking movements lent them the appearance of some
sort of circus act. Yet a brooding menace that hung
around them made me certain that they were not here
solely for entertainment.
One of the female members tugged at her shift and
stepped from it as it fell to the floor. I smirked and
ducked further into the grass as she swayed against one
of the men; here rounded belly glistening with the rest
of her flesh with some rainbow tinged oil that seemed
to sparkle in the yellow, briny sun.
She dropped to her hands and feet and scuttled into the
water, mouth agape, tongue lolling and eyes seemingly
forced almost from their sockets. She turned back to the
group and began swaying again, her lower half
submerged in the water and causing waves that
popped new bubbles of gas across the pond, adding to
the foul stink.
The male thing responded. I felt slightly sickened now
but confess that the thought of running away was

stilled by the fear of being seen and not hampered by a
little intrigue at what was going on.
The man unslung his braces and raised each foot to
remove both his trousers and worn, unlaced boots;
dropping them where he stood.
His mate called to him from the pond;
"Ki! Ki! Ki! Ki! Ki!", a rasping, choking sound like a
thing that is throttled or gasping for air.
He removed his shirt from over his head and revealed
glistening flanks of the same rainbow hue. His oily skin
stretched tightly over his oddly formed rib cage. He too
dropped to all fours and scurried to the pond's flatulent
fascination.
The pair gyrated side by side, slapping midriffs and
rumps against one another and raising their heads
towards their comrades on the grass tufts that clacked
and played that dreadful air.
"Ki! Ki! Ki! Ki! Ki!"
"Ia, Cuchulchag! Cuchulchag! ftaghn", the group's
voice cried in a croaking calumny of a choral response.
The pair batted together for a moment longer and then
both froze, shivering as if stunned. I could not see their
faces but I knew their features were set and those
bulbous eyes glazed. They stayed still, only the
occasional twitch, for what seemed like a minute or so
before both suddenly lurched from the water, now
hunched like primates as they moved towards their
clothes.
My eyes were drawn toward the now settling parts of
the pond that they had left. Something slithered there
and lapped at the surface of the water, before pushing
itself further towards the dark centre of the pool.
I shivered at the very sight of those ripples upon the

water.

Whatever those things were, they joined me in being startled by the sound of a bicycle bell from the nearby road. Over the desiccated wooden gate, no longer any real form of barrier, my father stood. Tall and imposing in his police uniform and police bicycle leaning against his side.

The travellers moved off down the field toward the shoreline, the less dressed holding their ragged clothes against the odd coloured flesh that was revealed below. Bulbous eyes staring dispassionately at my father who glared at them with some level of disgust.

I followed as surreptitiously as I could, squelching through the thick mud that was squashed between the clumps of grass.

"On your rounds again, Officer"? I knew that voice, it belonged to Raul Stanley, a local landowner of some infamy amongst my parents. Whose wild, bacchanalian parties were said to be held in the small disused castle (really a folly) that stood opposite the large imposing children's tuberculosis hospital on the seafront.

Rumour had it that the earls of Derby had started the fashion for those raucous weekend revelries in the late seventeenth century when horse races were held along the front and copious amounts of wine and revelry would lead to wild dancing and alien, incomprehensible ululations and roars that would hover among the damp, misty streets of the town in the still of night. Occasionally a scream might intersperse the odd, otherworldly noises as I pulled the blankets over my face to block out the hubbub.

Stanley was a tall, lean man; sporting jet black hair and cruel, glaring grey eyes. He was given to flamboyance, often carrying a cane or crop for effect. Yet this man was no actor or theatrical. His demeanour revealed a cruel sadistic mien; made all too clear by his sardonic sneers and flared nostrils.

"You seem to be interested in my visitors I see"? Stanley's nose wrinkled in contempt.

"Visitors Mr Stanley"? My father turned to look at him further down the lane. "Strange visitors you'd invite onto your land sir, ones that'd commit lewdness in public".

"Hardly public, Officer. It's private property and my land, now how about you turn your little cycle about and push awff back to your desk and a nice cup of tea". If my friends happen upon the public lane, then I'll call you"

"I'll be keeping an eye on those friends of yours Mr Stanley", he turned to the travellers as they crept, supinely, toward their protector, "you can be sure I'll be keeping an eye on you".

Stanley snarled at him and struck his riding crop against his mud spattered gaiters.

"Bidding you a good afternoon Mr Stanley". He mounted his cycle and moved off up the lane slowly. Once he was out of earshot I could hear the landowner chastising the travellers, both sharing that odd guttural language. Their conversation ended with them looking back to where my father was just turning the end of the lane and the group nodding and grinning as one.

I shuddered.

Chapter Two

The town school was a ramshackle affair. A run down, mould encrusted prefab which offered a few cold, damp rooms, odd legged chairs and hand-me-down desks with black, gaping lobotomy-hole inkwells. With asbestos walls and asbestos ceilings, the entire edifice seemed to sag and list as the few pupils walked in and out of the few rooms. My teacher there was Miss Harker, a plain but prim woman in her early twenties and obviously relatively new to the position. Perhaps she had arrived in the summer holidays before I began to attend the school?

It was shortly after my hidden reconnaissance by the millpond; the memories of the millpond were long. The grandparents of the children that had gone missing there had deceased a long time ago, *yet the millpond still seemed to remember…* that the familiar stooped figure of Rob Daniel came into the classroom during one of the many 'copy from the blackboard' sessions that were presented to us. He made his way slowly toward Miss Harker, eyes darting at me as he moved across the bowing floor. The other children, all six of them, each with the same pallid wet complexion and yellowed, bulbous eyes turned to stare at me. One of the girls at the front even made a leer at me as her overbite emerged and left a small trickle of drool that ran down the edge of her mouth.

Daniel stopped for a short while to whisper something to Miss Harker that I could not quite catch. It was only when he turned to look at me and she lowered her head to look over her glasses at me that the subject of their parley was me. My face flushed as the other children turned away from me as Daniel exited the room.

I was not sure what had just happened. What had been said about me? Did I have any sort of recourse or opportunity to rebut whatever claims were made. Nothing else was said of the matter as the hand bell rang to signal end of school that day. Miss Harker did not even look at me as we left. Just the usual points and whispers of the other odd looking classmates.

It was as I was leaving the gate though that the hairs on the nape of my neck stood up and it became all too obvious I was being looked at by someone behind me. I turned, surreptitiously, to try and observe my observer and locked eyes with a figure on a bicycle that was some fifty feet up the road. He was wrapped up in a thick overcoat with a short piece of rope for a belt and his head sported a bent out of shape felt hat that dripped the drizzle away from his pallid, yellow-green face and dark, swollen eyes. Was that thing watching me? Was that thing even alive?

I hastened away, keeping my eyes down, more in fear of what was behind me than in protection from the rain. As I walked past the Coach and Horses Inn I turned again. He was there. Stopped, his hand on a wall next to a road sign on the other side of the road that led to the coast. The short pavement, left cigarette stubs from the patrons, the mould encrusted pebble dashed front of the inn and its dirty unkempt windows hiding dirty, unkempt curtains. I began to panic, what was I doing here? This was no place for me.

I turned again and ran now. Ran for home, for the safety of the fireplace, the heavy door and my parents. All the while I could hear the distant clicking of the

chain as the cyclist kept the same distance behind me.
I said nothing to my mother as I hurriedly cleaned my
plate that evening. I was too full of trepidation at what
I might see when I went to my room and looked out of
the window. I could see the cyclist now in my mind's
eye, collars turned up and hat pulled down; shielding
that jaundiced pallor and gawping muzzle from the
drizzle.
As I closed the door to my room I heard the front door
close below me. I looked out of the window and saw
nothing, no cyclist, no learer at the end of the lane; only
the eel-like runnels of grimy water that slithered down
the pane. My father had arrived home. In doing so I
assumed he had caused the odd creature to stalk back
to its hiding place.

Chapter Three

It took no great effort to overhear my parents, the house was so small all I really needed to do was hold the door ajar with my foot as I lay on my bed. My father's words echoed easily up the stairs in his sonorous, Lancastrian legato; my mother's less so in her softer, less regional accent.
He had sat down at the dining table to take his boots off and tug at the toes of his socks.
My mother failed to comment. Something was seriously amiss.
"I mean to have that scoundrel, and I mean to haul him in for a quick word tonight", My father tried his best to keep his voice from bouncing off the walls with no luck whatsoever.
"What did Leonard say"? That was my mother's voice, Leonard was my father's boss, Sergeant Leonard Menzies, an old veteran of the police service, put out here in the sticks to graze until retirement. He was cautious and keen to make sure his last few years of service went as smoothly as possible.
"What do you think he said? If I have evidence of illegal activity, then I should present it and let the law do the rest. He's scared, scared of Stanley and his henchmen".
"He has every right to be. You know he all but controls this place".
"We all know that, but you've heard those sounds at night on the seafront, something isn't right and I intend to find out"
"You'll shake up trouble. You're putting a stick in a wasps' nest"

"Aye, where's the lad? He upstairs"?
"He is, how he sleeps with all the noise you make is beyond me"
"Sleep? It's barely dark lass, I'll finish my tea and go and say g'night to the lad".
"Do you think he's been having those dreams about the city underwater? The ones *they* have"?
They? Who was *they*?
"That's idle talk, you know what comes from straining your ears and hiding behind shelves in corner shops", my father snorted.
"I've told you. They all have the same dream. I heard them talking about it. The sunken city".
"Rubbish, if the lad had dreams like that he'd tell you, or he'd be so tired you'd notice. Leave that superstitious claptrap to the locals".
"It may be unnatural and superstitious but they believe it".
"People believe in all sorts of rubbish", he set his tea mug down and stood up, stretching; I could hear the crack of his shoulders. Then the familiar soft plod of his feet against the stair runner.
"You reading those comics in this dim light again lad? You'll look like a mole in the morning".
I grinned at the preposterous thought.
He moved to the window and looked out slowly, carefully.
"Looks like there'll be nasty storms tonight. You make sure this window is closed tight. You know how it rattles in the wind. We can't afford to fix it if it breaks".
He fastened the lock tight against the bottom sash window. His hand was shaking. I could just about notice it.

"I've got to go out on business again in an hour or so lad so I want you to make sure you look after your Mam if it gets too blustery or the thunder gets too loud. You know how she thinks this place will come tumbling down around us", he smiled down and ruffled my hair.
"I will Dad, I will".
He left my room and didn't turn, as if it was the last time I would ever see him.
It wasn't.

Chapter Four

It was past nine when my father left the house. It was a familiar sound to hear him wrestling with the heavy cape he wore to protect him from the elements, considering the blustering wind outside and the rain hammering against the window he would need it.
I had my own thick, felt coat and woollen hat hidden under my bed for my nocturnal sojourn too. I had to know what was going on in this weird place.
With the click of the door latch downstairs I waited for my mother to settle down to her reading and then fumbled with coat and hat to get them on in the near Cimmerian darkness. I had tied my boot laces together and draped them over my shoulder. The hobnails would make way too much noise up here and a pair of wet socks really wouldn't be my worst worry considering the weather outside. I am back right there as I recount this, the look of my hand, pale against the moonlight, as I opened the sliding lock on the window and drew the sash up as quietly as I could. The gasp as the bitterly cold rain lashed at my face and neck as I clambered through the frame onto the greasy slates. The grimace on my face as I shimmied the window from side to side to drop it closed again.
It was a simple slide down the slates and a drop of eight feet that deposited me on the pavement outside our house. I looked left and right and saw there was no one about; at least no one I could see in the pelting rain and squalling wind.
I donned my boots and headed into town, shoulders hunched and hands thrust into pockets like some nefarious Victorian footpad.

I knew where my father would go first. The Coach and Horses. If he worked at night like this, he always stopped in for a tot to keep him warm and a chance to catch the mood of the few people that frequented the place in the evening.

I was not disappointed, there he was. A towering figure, with a tiny whisky, talking to five or six patrons at the bar. By the looks of their hunched frames and narrowed eyes they were discussing something that didn't care to be overheard too.

I pulled the drenched hat back from my face as the rain battered down against me. I had to get into some cover that would allow me to see what was happening outside the pub. I couldn't stand out here in the rain for another minute.

I ran across the lane to a small group of trees and huddled at the base of them whilst the roaring of thunder began to erupt across the Irish sea and the blue-white tridents of electricity shot across the sky. I was shocked by the raw power that overawed me as I crouched there amid the waterfalls of rain that leapt from the leaves.

It seemed like an age that I had remained motionless, a silent watcher beneath the moonlit beams of the trees, occasionally illumined by the flashes in the air like one of the silent movie stars I had heard of.

My father emerged from the inn with six men in tow, earnest and determined, despite the rain, as they pulled up their collars and marched along the pasture lane that headed to the coast.

Chapter Five

The empty streets, battered by sheets of heavy rain and shrouded by the angry clouds and of hidden moon, made a ready hiding place for a young lad so inquisitive. I followed my father and his small gang along the lane, keeping at a safe distance and darted from cover to cover. They kept a fast pace; some filled with a spirit of enmity or indignation and a couple just full of spirits. None of them were local to place, how could they be? *They didn't even look like the locals!*
It was obvious that they were headed towards the lighthouse, the only place they could be going this far towards the coast, there was only the abandoned castle and the large, hideous looking TB hospital this close to the coast. They splashed through the calf depth water as I followed covering my face against the foul smelling liquid we were forcing our feet through and the stinging rain that pelted my face.
A blaze of lightning lit up the end of the lane where a group of men were waiting. Wrapped in thick overcoats and oilskins. Each armed with a cruel club which some used as a stick as if to steady them in the downpour.
There was a brief exchange between the two groups. I could almost hear what my father said. His voice boomed out despite the rain. The other men hefted their clubs and stepped forward. As their leader placed a hand on my father's I saw the flash of a knife appear from beneath his oilskins and I heard a loud shriek as his truncheon came down heavily on that arm. My father brought the truncheon up again and sent it crashing down onto his assailant's shoulder. He fell to

the ground.

Two of my father's men broke and ran, no stomach to face the clubs that were now flailing into the melee. Another two fell in short order, one with a club to the face which left the man minus a few teeth and bereft of consciousness, his body dropping to the lane with a splash, and another who took a hit straight to the torso which took the wind straight out of him. My father's last comrade fought bravely by his side, his fists seemed to be clubs of their own, until he was floored by a cruel blow to the back of the head that left him collapsing in pain as blood mixed with the rain that gushed down his back.

My father held his own for a while, the truncheon flailed wildly dropping one then two of his assailants. It was only when one of the oilskin wearing gang members leapt at him and got his hands around my father's neck that the others moved in and struck heavy blows into his chest and legs. After a few seconds his fighting stopped and he became still, slumping against the floor to be dragged by the collar by one of the ruffians.

I scowled and cursed at the cowards that were still visible, skulking away down the flooded lane back to town. As the gang dragged my father and their own injured colleagues toward the waiting light of the lighthouse I crept behind them and surveilled my father's fallen that were coughing or trying to pick themselves up. One appeared to be drowning in the shallow, foul water. I turned him over and placed his head on a kerb. Lifting his mouth clear of the rank run off from the flood land. There beside him I saw the glimmer of the knife that the gang member had pulled on my father; a cruel snake like blade adorned on the hilt with ichthyic castings that curved to bite one another at the intersection with the handle. I looked about me and pocketed the thing, pressing on in the hope of helping my father.

The lane that led to the lighthouse turned left and crested rough ground that fell into rutted, flooded ditches, some deep enough to drown a man, I had to keep my eyes upon my father's captors as well as on the narrow path that was hard to see with the sheets of rain and sloshing water around me.

It was this division of attention that must have led me to oversee the looming figure beside me as it hovered and then pounced. It was all I could do to stagger and retain my footing as the oil skinned thing lifted itself up from the muddied ground, its felt hat slipping in the rain and falling to the floor.

I gasped both in revulsion and terror. It was the cyclist who had been following; now made plain for me to see. Its, I won't say his, face was mottled with dark patches, the thunderous sky precluded details. The eyes were bulbous and yellow, unblinking and that maw was all too familiar, long and thin, drooping into an absence of chin or any real neck. Its head was sloped upward, elongated like some form of alien mitre. Wholly inhuman and yet containing some blasphemous mockery of the man it once was.

I remained rigid, struck paralysed by what I was confronted with.

The creature made another lunge at me, this time attempting to rend my face with its pitted, rotten talons. I moved aside and winced as it scraped past my cheek tearing the flesh with a sickening sound that was more felt than heard as the rain pounded.

I reached into my pocket, drawing the knife that was there and brandished it at the thing. Half expecting to be dead in the next ten seconds. The shock of what was happening was still pumping the adrenaline around my body, keeping me capable of doing whatever I could to get out of this alive.

It tilted its head at the sight of the knife, first in recollection and then in ire. The thing flew at me, enraged. Its arms flailing and making a screeching sound that was loud even above the rain and crashing waves.

Using its own indignation against it, feeling it hands grapple around my throat, and stabbed the knife into where its neck should have been. First once, then twice and finally one last time as it croaked an awful sound and collapsed to the ground. The rain battered at the thing as its greyish green blood hissed from the newly created extra gills in its neck. I glared at it in horror and then turned to release my supper across the sodden ground; fear finally catching up with me.

I had not time to think as I pressed on, no time to ditch the creature in a pool or similar. Only time to steal back the dagger and secret it in my pocket.

As I crested the slippy, grimy sandstone that led up to the lighthouse I could see my father being dragged from the place, his face bloodied and head bobbing in the merest of consciousness. He had been stripped of his shirt and boots and wore only his trousers. There was a large welt across his back seemingly caused by the claw of a large creature. They heaved him over to a large, heavy wooden table that was laid out amongst the rising waves of the shoreline and secured him to the beams of the legs with ropes. There followed another figure from the lighthouse now, dressed in long aquamarine robes that shimmered in the dim light like the scales of a fish caught in the angler's light. By the swagger I knew who it was instantly.

Raul Stanley. That cruel libertine that had threatened my father not so long ago.

It was obvious to me that they meant to watch my father perish beneath the waves of the sea in some strange undinal offering. I thought it more than likely that they would do that out of the storm and out of the battering rain and squalls of the shoreline.

Heads bobbed and surfaced as a crowd rose from the oily sand gravel of the shoreline. How many of the townspeople had been seated down there, unmoving and silent? I hadn't even noticed them.

They raised their hands into the air, screaming and grunting, yelling and clacking in some alien tongue, intoning into the vast grey, foaming swell of the furious sea;

"Ia, Cuchulchag! Cuchulchag!
Ph'nglui mglw'nafh
Cthulhu R'lyeh wgah-nagl ftaghn!"

On the last shout the sky erupted in a massive roar of energy, lightning blistered the sky as a near simultaneous, juddering blast of thunder threatened to send me from my feet.

The dagger, clutched within Stanley's cuff till needed, struck into my father's chest and tore down into his lower abdomen.

Blood sprayed, mixing with the dirty foam of the sea.

"Daaaaaaaaaa", I roared and then dropped to my knees. Eyes stinging with rain and tears.

"Noooo".

The roar of the sea, the shrieking wind and the biting rain rendered my protests mute. I turned and headed back the way I had come; my father's request for me to look after my mother burning in my ears. I tried to run as much of it as I could, but most of it was just too flooded to make quick progress. It seemed like an age when I arrived back at the house, waterlogged and covered in grime and spots of my own blood.
I had pounded at the door until my mother had opened it, still fully dressed and rubbing her eyes from fatigue. She had remained in vigil for my father to get back. The look on my face and the cruel cuts across my cheek gave her her answer.
We never spoke until we were gone. She left that place as bereft of belongings as I. Her, with an old grey blanket she used to cover herself from the rain, and I with the dagger I had found on the pasture lane. She never looked back. I did. To see some of the townspeople banging on our door. With my father's truncheon.

Chapter Six

I never lived near the sea again. The Midlands of England, where I spent my life until today, were far enough from the sound of gulls and spray for me to feel far enough away.

It was only when I arrived here in Aberystwyth, this morning, with you and your Mum that I felt the need to write any of this down. A tale that has not crossed my lips in eighty years. Yet, when we arrived here, the smell of the briny air and the chilling sound of the waves rekindled in me a need to tell someone what passed in that town so many years ago.

When the landlady of this bed and breakfast regarded me with those bulbous, yellow unblinking eyes, with something almost approaching recognition. When I turned as we walked away with our keys and she was still staring at me whilst talking on the 'phone, it sparked so many memories.

So I set these words down for you in my unsteady prose, with my unsteady hands. What little I can remember. A tall tale for my youngest, but most inquisitive grandson. I enclose in this package that dagger from the place, as gleaming and sharp as the terrible day I found it. I hope you will not look back at me as some old fool.

I'll sign off, there's someone banging on the door. People are so impatient nowadays!

Round

He had not slept at all that night. The very idea of downsizing had begun to nag at him. They had both decided that the move from the city was what they wanted. A chance to flee from their humdrum office jobs and the daily commute. She to concentrate on her sales of jewellery and he to take up his childhood dream of the task of a milkman.

A self-employed milkman at that. The round was all his own. He found the customers (well, the previous owner of the round did, at least), kept them happy and then reaped the rewards at the end of the week when he could sleep in on a Sunday morning.

They had downsized at just the right time, as the house prices kept steady in the town whilst demand in the country had fallen. The sale of their house had provided both of them with a two storey detached home, two new cars and a milk round. They had spent the last two decades creaming it in, now they would spend the remainder delivering cream to others, at least Miles would.

Yet here he was now looking out of the back kitchen window with a mix of fear and a deep, guilty regret that he had allowed this experiment to happen. Neither of them were particularly adventurous but Miles had always liked to think he was level headed at least. Why then had he given up the well paid managerial job with the man to become a milkman? *A milkman?*

It had been six months ago when they had taken that drive into the country and had spotted this place, a small village full of old houses, well maintained by the old residents, still not overtaken by the commuters; bankers, solicitors and accountants that slowly chewed at little locales like these.
He had not even checked on the viability of the round before taking it on. Of course, he had followed the route in his car and pored over his road atlas to familiarise himself with the area but, for all he knew, the outlay might be horrendous. He knew how much he had to pay the dairy for the use of the float's charging and parking and the base price of the milk but what if there were other costs he did not know about?

He had friends back in the town too. He used to play squash. Now he'd be delivering it. No more afternoon gins at the sports club on Sundays. No more lunches at the Kings Arms on a Wednesday, no more flirting with the girls from accounts on the way to kettle and tea area.
He straightened his tie, smoothed back a stray eyebrow hair and tilted his hat back slightly, milkmen always had their hat tilted back.

As he set off from their drive at in the darkness of that 2.00AM start he thought to himself that no one would ever recognise him in his new outfit. Oddly enough, to anyone who would have been awake to pay him any attention he looked exactly like a middle manager pretending to be a milkman.

He eschewed the MP3 player in favour of the local

radio station which was playing some syndicated nonsense which mixed all the latest chart hits with a steady stream of traffic reports, celebrity gossip and mind-numbing tittle tattle from its presenter 'Johnny Chase'. It was a late spring morning, warm and quiet, still dark but promising a stunning dawn, as he left his drive and headed out, keeping his engine revs low to avoid awakening his neighbours.

The dairy was only ten minutes away, on the outskirts of the next village on the other side of the hill. His car joined a small column of three as they entered the gate to the dairy's car park. It was fortunate that he had fallen in behind the other cars as he was uncertain as to where he was supposed to park.

Miles pretended to look at his phone as he watched the others head toward the dairy's main door and enter, the door was ill fitting and showed the orange light from beneath its base which was caught up in a coconut mat. He exited his car and hurried into the dairy building to ensure he could follow the routine that the others would be carrying out.
The other milkmen were busy carrying their crates to their floats, occasionally pausing to swap small quips and turning to look at the awkward newcomer.
Miles walked straight to the stack of crates that bore the number for his round, printed clearly on a fresh sheet of A4 and laminated. Obviously, the previous owner of his round needed no such sign. Miles felt awkward and a little embarrassed.
Dead men's shoes.
He avoided the inquisitive glances that shot his way as

he hefted the crates and carried them out, through the open back doors to the waiting float outside. He had already seen the old float when he took over the round and recognised it instantly.

It was with a little relief that Miles loaded the last crate on board, checked his itinerary and started the float out of the gates of the dairy. As he moved out onto the main road and headed back to his village his tensions eased and he began to feel a little more settled, the first notes of the dawn chorus were rising from the still air and the still slumbering sun was beginning to make his presence felt over to the East.

Though he had not been in the village for long he had memorised the layout of the sixty or so houses very well using a map. It was easy to navigate the course of his deliveries here and his mood was lifted by the first songs of the birds in the hedgerows. Perhaps he had made the right choice after all? The morning was idyllic.

The light across the fields and the lane he was driving was now at the full glow of the sunrise as he trundled his milk float toward the outermost delivery on his round. For a mere two pints of milk it was a long distance to cover outside his main round, it was likely that someone had tacked this delivery onto his round before he started as it was too remote for most of the others too. Maybe he could have a word with the householders at the end of the week and convince them to up their delivery items. Sales was a large part of what he used to do for a living. Getting a few pounds' worth of deliveries every week might pay for the inconvenience of travelling out this far every morning. It was an odd location for a house. It must have been built at a time when the surrounding fields were populated by workers and the lanes clattered with horses' hooves and cart wheels. Now it was a relic of a past that was drowned beneath the roar of the motorway only a few hundred yards away. No road led to the arterial route that roared and coughed behind the property, the high trees and bushes around the house seemed to have been planted to shut out the world that had changed the rural backdrop of the dwelling forever.

As Miles pulled the milk float to a halt to turn into the drive of the house a squirrel scampered across the opening of the drive and regarded him briefly before hopping its way past the opposite gatepost and back into the trees.

Miles smiled.

As he guided the float onto the driveway he became aware of just how much shielding from the outside sounds the trees that lined the property provided. It was eerily silent in the confines of the wooded wall, it was only the sunrise poking through the coniferous crenulations that reminded him that it was daybreak. It could almost be a languid summer's evening as he looked across the trimmed lawns and well-tended flower beds.

The house was hardly the dwelling place of some tenant or peasant farmer. It was a Victorian affair of three stories, probably a rectory at some point. It had that prim and well maintained properness about the property. A lush, verdant lawn was framed by the gravel drive and many well-tended flower beds that glistened in the morning dew.

The float made short work of dispelling this peaceful

scene as it trundled along the loose gravel drive. Even with the cover of the trees to his side Miles felt slightly ridiculous as his vehicle crunched and ground its way along the drive to the large house.

It was something of a relief to pull up outside the door of the residence and he halted for a few seconds to let the ringing of the tyres on the drive retreat from his ears.

He grabbed at two pint bottles as he made his way around the back of the float, almost as if he had done it many times before. With a short, brisk stride he attained the front door and placed the full bottles of milk into the sturdy, wire bottle holder. It was only as he got close to the covered porch of the doorway that he saw that the dark blue door was not plastic, as he had thought, but painted wood. Painted so well that the surface almost looked like glass. The window to his side was the same. Superbly painted by a master craftsman. He noticed the slender carved oak branches that snaked up the wooden columns that held up the portico, painted equally beautifully.

As he got back to his float Miles returned an admiring glance back to this most handsome of houses. As he did so he fancied he saw one of the drapes move back into place rapidly behind the third storey window. The residual movement of the curtain seemed to confirm it. Someone was watching his delivery from the upstairs window. Miles became suddenly conscious of his prying, like a child caught peeping through a keyhole. He clambered back into the float and moved back along the drive wincing as the gravel crunched again beneath his tyres.

Turning back toward the dairy, his morning's round

now finished, he felt a sense of achievement. His first day's delivery done and he had not got lost, had got all the orders correct and had even found out how to get to this most remote of delivery points.

Even the roar of the nearby motorway failed to drown out his off-key whistling as he guided the float back for a recharge.

Chapter Two

He slept easily that evening. Kissing wife goodnight at seven in the evening so he could rise at one thirty in the morning did seem a little odd but he was sure it would become routine soon enough. His head had been serenely still as he drifted off to sleep. The very idea of being so stress free would never have seemed possible a few months ago.

He dreamed of that house, he was standing by the entrance to the drive and looking across the lawn to the upper window except the window had gone and had been replaced with a solitary eye that looked down at him in contempt. A rolling storm of clouds emerged from the back of the house and began to creep across the sky, shrouding the place in darkness as he watched. The birds cried and took flight as the storm clouds cleared the front of the building and moved across the garden.

Miles opened his eyes and lay still for a moment as his awareness returned. An odd dream to have considering how relaxed he had been. The room was dark and his wife was beside him breathing steadily in sleep. He checked his watch. It was almost one in the morning. He might as well get up.

The toast popping from the toaster brought him back to consciousness again as the kettle finally boiled. With a yawn and a scratch of the head he set his breakfast down at the dining table and retrieved his phone from his dressing gown. His fascination with the house was far from waning.

It was a tortuous route to find the house on his phone's maps application. The hedgerows seemed lower and the lighting seemed dimmer when the street view had been taken four years ago. He was quite surprised that the camera car had even bothered to drive down that silent road to nowhere.

His discovery was somewhat lacklustre. The trees surrounding the house were overgrown, a small view of an untended lawn, now more a meadow, was visible through the entrance and the drive had been tarmac back then and not gravel, Its lumpen face pockmarked by protruding patches of grass and shrubbery.

The only object that did seem to correspond to any order was the purple and white 'For Sale' sign that was attached to a pole beside the road.

Miles looked back at the date of the page; four years ago. Whoever had bought the house had made a very good job of tidying everything up and restoring the property to its former excellence.

Miles had to wonder though;

'exactly who would want that kind of isolation and yet be happy to live next door to a roaring motorway'?

He looked up at the clock on the corner of his phone. He was running late.

Despite only having the most cursory of showers and a far from substantial brush of his teeth, Miles set out from the dairy in something of a fine mood. The weather was spectacular again. Warm enough to be pleasant at this time of the morning (or night, depending on your sleep pattern) and promising another sunny, bright day ahead.

As his float trundled its way toward the house at the end of his round, making its quiet way toward the noisy motorway, he pondered on the woodland that surrounded the road. Just how old was it? Some parts

of it seemed to have been there forever; ancient fallen
tree trunks covered in equally old moss. Verdant ferns
that seemed to be right out of the Jurassic period
nestled amongst the tangles of thickets, brambles and
blackberries. One could almost imagine a few, hardy
Cornovii warriors still sitting somewhere in there,
unaware that the Roman invasion was over.
The trees thinned out and the familiar fields took over
the roadside as Miles approached the house. The sun
was rising again on its leisurely way to its zenith and
casting a fine, comfortable glow across the damp
grasses.
He navigated the float up to the driveway and stopped.
He had remembered the gravel disaster of yesterday.
He was not getting caught in that noisy louse up again.
Miles retrieved the two pints of milk from the back of
the float and began to walk up the drive, attempting to
make as little noise as he could as his shoes nestled
themselves into the tiny shingle. He could walk on the
lawn, quieter but disrespectful. Miles was not the sort
of milkman to traverse another man's lawn.
As he arrived at the house he cast a glance at the very
top window to see if his viewer was waiting. The
drapes were still and half parted. There was insufficient
light to see into the room so far.
He placed the two bottles into the wire holder, noted
that the empties had not been placed out for his
collection and added a quick note to this fact in his little
notebook.
The exquisitely painted door held his attention again
for a moment. He could actually see himself in the
reflection now. A little distorted but still it was
obviously him. How on earth could someone get paint

to apply like that?

He backed away from the portal, shaking his head at the workmanship and headed back down the drive to his float. As he did so, he looked up at the large bay window above the door. There was a woman there staring at him. She was young, maybe in her early twenties and dressed in white, perhaps some cotton nightgown that matched her pale, alabaster face. Her hair was long and a dark brown that matched her eyes, at least as far as Miles could ascertain at this distance and in this light.

Her hand was holding the cord that held the raised blinds from falling back to the floor. Her other hand toyed at the glass as if she was uncertain as to whether she wanted to communicate with him. Her face, quite beautiful in its symmetry, seemed equally noncommittal.

She turned, the long billowing sleeves of her gown swaying as she moved. Her eyes came back to him and fixed him where he stood. They were open in warning, in an unspoken conveyance of a threat that was imminent. Her free hand made a faint gesture for him to leave as the blinds dropped suddenly and she was gone.

When he had reached his vehicle he stopped briefly, retrieved his phone and snapped some images of the house from the seat of the float.

Intriguing.

Chapter Three

Armed with the knowledge of the estate agent's details from the sign on his map app, Miles called them as soon as he guessed they would be open. He was disappointed by the news, from a young receptionist who was probably still at school when the house was last on the market, that there was no information about the house retained on the company's database. He placed the handset back in the cradle with the thought that he had no reason to be so inquisitive about that odd house. Perhaps in the few weeks he had lived in the little village he had acclimatised to the way of life, its attention to little details and incongruities.

His night's sleep was broken yet again by dreams of the house. The trees that formed its boundaries had seemingly become gelatinous, slithering into the shapes of myriad tentacles, each slowly reaching into the air to fall to the damp ground under their weight. An obscene slap greeted their contact with the earth which made a repulsive thumping which could be felt by the feet.

The house itself had taken on an aspect of a most geometrically affronting condition. Its sides seemed to meld with each other and its front looped hither and thither with its back, whilst still retaining its basic rectangular character.

The whole milieu left him feeling sickened and startled. As he began to panic that eyes open eyes could not find a place to point that did not leave him feeling overawed and disgusted he happened upon the middle window in which he had seen the woman. It was fortunate that the dimensions of the window

maintained their regularity and gave his staring eyes
something to focus on, but the pane itself was as black
as space. A cold, empty vacuum of entropy. Yet what
was that? Something deep within the blackness
flickered and sputtered, a flame was it? Or a circle of
flame, some odd mythological mandala of fire?
It was gone as soon as it had started and Miles awake
with a start himself. His pillow soaked with sweat and
his mouth as parched as papyrus. His wife stirred and
grumbled as she turned over away from him.
He left the bedroom and headed downstairs for his
breakfast, his watch told him it was one AM again. At
this rate he would not need to set his alarm any more.
He felt chilled as he clambered down the stairs half
asleep. Perhaps the dream had shaken him more than
he though? Or perhaps it was just cold this morning.
He had consumed his tea and toast mindlessly at the
breakfast bar. Even the perky radio presenter failed to
spur his mind into any sort of action. He was feeling
dog tired and a little burnt bread and caffeine was not
remedying the situation.
He was almost leaden when he arrived at the dairy, on
time surprisingly. He had even nodded at his fellow
milkmen despite their grins and whisperings. It was as
an automaton that he exited the gates on his float, his
round penned out in front of him on his little notepad.
As he jumped to and from his seat, the bottles of his
wares clanking as he brought back the empties and
joining with the gradual birdsong, he began to awaken.
It must have been the exercise that enlivened him, that
and the clear, fresh air of the morning. Within ten
minutes he was whistling, and the fatigue of earlier was
a mere bagatelle. His little float hummed to him as it

trundled along the lanes out of the last village and onto the narrow minor road that led to the house by the motorway.

Miles stopped the float at the entrance again and grabbed the two pints of milk for the delivery. As he did so he took out his phone and snapped a few photographs of the tree lined garden and one of the house. He supposed it was a way of solidifying the place in case his dream was more accurate than he expected.

As he entered the garden the sound of the motorway rush receded again to be replaced by silence. The muffling cover of the trees really was impressive. It was almost like moving from a busy street into some necropolis, a place of silence and reverence amidst a tumult of noise and tension.

He began the trek along the drive as usual, the gravel crunching beneath his feet to make an embarrassing din. His eyes were fixed on the house, particularly the middle window where he had seen the woman the day before.

It was still, there was no movement at any of the windows, and all the drapes were shut tight.

He placed the bottles down on the step and noted that the empties had not been left outside again. Maybe they stored the things up until the weekend?

It was as he was leaving the step and about to head back along the path that he had the alarming feeling that he was being watched from the house.

Only when I turn and look back, he thought.

He did so, craning his neck around nervously to look straight into the downstairs bay window. The drapes were wide open and inside, illuminated by a mass of flickering candles was a tall, black man. His skin was jet, darker than any human flesh. It glistened with a smooth sheen as the candlelight played with the features of his face. He was clad in a dark robe of some shimmering cloth, embroidered hieroglyphs stood out at the collar and cuffs crafted in a glistening gold. The creature's, for it was no man, eyes were obsidian, set in sclerae of a spoiled, bloody crimson.

It stood watching him, grinning. A leering, menacing smirk that chilled him. Its hand was pointing. Pointing upward from where it stood.

Miles followed its directions and found his gaze fixed now on the middle window of the house again. The woman was there, at the window, striking at the panes in silence, no sound issuing from her warnings. She mouthed something, seemingly shouting, yet Miles could hear nothing.

He backed away in alarm, even the beauty of the woman could not mask the wholly unnatural sequence of events.

He faced front again and began to run back to the drive's entrance. Not turning back. His gasping, fearful breaths came to him in rasping panic as he got back to his float and turned to look back at the house. Everything seemed quiet again.

He snatched his phone from his pocket, his hands shaking now, opened the camera app and zoomed in on the front of the house. All the drapes were closed again and there was no sign of that odd apparition in the dark robes.

The tangible feel of the float and the faint sound of the motorway traffic now he was almost out of the grounds of the house steeled him a little. Whatever was going

on up there was sinister to say the least and involved a young woman that was calling for his help. Chivalry might be dead but Miles maintained at least a working association with civic duty. He had to at least try to help her before calling the authorities.
He set the float in motion and headed back toward the house along the drive. This time the noise of the gravel barely even registered.
As he stopped the float outside the porch he left the driver's seat and drew himself up to full height, walking confidently toward the door. Noting that all the drapes were drawn again.
It was a confident knock, well, more of a thump, on the mirror finished door that made it pop open and slowly move ajar with a creak.
A sweet, bilious odour wafted past him.
"Hello"? He called out.

Miles Thompson was reported missing by his wife the after he had failed to show up for his milk delivery round. After a police search of the area was carried out with nothing found it had been assumed that he had simply taken off to another location, probably with someone he had met at his former employment.
It was only when a vagrant reported his milk float as being abandoned by a house near the motorway, a few miles from the dairy, that any suspicion of foul play had been entertained.
The float had been left outside the house, empty of full bottles of milk but stacked with empty bottles (so the driver's round had been completed), the keys to the float were still in the ignition and the driver's phone and notebook were still in the cab.

The notepad mentioned that the driver had indeed visited the location and noted that empty milk bottles had not been placed on the step. Oddly there were six full bottles of spoiled milk sitting on the step when police searched the location.

The phone contained a number of photographs of the boarded up house, including a couple that had been taken with a shaky hand at the end of the pitted and badly cracked tarmac drive. In one, the 'for sale' sign (which had been removed from the outside of the property and thrown onto the overgrown and weed strewn lawn) was clearly visible in the murky light, proving that the photograph had been taken very early in the morning.

When police had opened and searched the house they had found nothing untoward except for some used candles and graffiti in the living room that had probably been left by the house's last occupants, a new age group from London, who had rented the property in the late nineties and were untraceable for the rent they had owed when they left.

Miles Thompson's whereabouts remain a mystery to this day.

Slithering Menace

The bungalow's single story was one of decay. Its window frames were brown and rotted, its oblong eyes yellowed with old, desiccated net curtains, hanging dishevelled behind grimed, unkempt glass. Its door of flaked varnish and mould, its grass gone beyond any form of upkeep or any form of repair. Hard, dry dead patches sat beside wild mixes of weeds and creeping shrubbery. The hedges that surrounded the property were now tangles of thick, often prickly, vines and branches of a species of tree which was most definitely not native to the area. The wall, once covered with pebbledash, had now lost most of its covering revealing its old, chipped decaying brick beneath. The gate had once been painted blue, but now had taken on the hue of both the garden and the house; a kind of sickly bilge green. The small letter box beyond the gate was testimony to the owner's fear of strangers, or at least his reticence for visitors. A rusty sign was pegged to its side;

NO HAWKERS, CANVASSERS OR TRESPASSERS-PLEASE DO NOT DISTURB.

This was the house of my old friend, Ashton Griffith, given to him by his grandfather. I had seen neither sight nor sound of him for a number of years and, as I was in the area, and had been asked by his sister, I took it upon myself to check on his wellbeing, or more rightly, to see if he was still alive.

The gate had lost its hinges and was merely propped up against the posts to bar entry to the property. I placed it back carefully as I entered. Mindful of the garden. I doubted any local animal that strayed onto the grass that had once been a lawn would ever find its way home again.

I walked to the dry, rotted door and inspected the aluminium letter box, now covered in grey, oxidised powder. Did the postman avoid this house? He can't just use the letterbox by the dysfunctional gate?

As I had noticed the door was original to the house, built in the 1950s and not painted or sanded in years. The unkempt appearance was evident with the window frames. Previously painted white, they were now a conglomeration of cream, brown and a dark green from mould.

I tried the bell, its off white plastic button encased in the same green matter, and, as expected, it failed to respond.

I knocked at the glass of the door three times, foolishly, as the rattle of the glass almost knocked away the rotted wooden trims, the putty had retreated a long time ago. There was no sound but I fancied I saw a shape wove about in the back of the building. The dim light inside was disturbed by the figure.

"Griffith, Griffith. It's me Blackwood. Can you hear me"? I knocked again. This time lightly on the wooden edge of the door. Still the glass rattled.

I checked through the marbled glass, there was definitely something moving there in the corridor. It was closer now, I could see an arm stretched up against the wall.

"Blackwood?" The voice was cracked through lack of use, almost as if the user had just awoken. Even my friend the eccentric Griffith rose before teatime.

"Blackwood, yes, of course. Is that you"?

"I just told you it was. Are you going to let me in"?
I moved my head to look at the single fish eye pane of glass in the centre of the door. I immediately wished I hadn't.
For, what was presented to me as the face of a friend I remembered as ruddy and beaming was something wholly different and unwholesome.
2.
Griffith opened the door a fraction and stared, or was that glared, at me. His eyes eventually narrowing to slits as he tried to overcome the painful light of the sun. His hair was a vivid white, as unkempt as his domicile and totally at odds with his age. He was in his late twenties just as I was, I recalled. His large hands were dry and the skin, paper thin; creased like anhydrous papyrus. His face was covered in a similar dried hide, akin to a skein of old, bleached cotton thread.
Two glaring eyes pierced me from beneath the wild, grass-like eyebrows. Still the same steely grey that they used to be, but now made bigger and more alarming both by the widening of the man's eyes and also by the incongruity between them and the surrounding flesh. The familiar red rings of sleep deprivation or ill health, the cracked dry lips amongst the white stubble of the pointed chin and the dirty pullover and trousers all pointed to a man that had forsaken the inconvenience of upkeep.
Even his bare, dirty feet, sat atop the threadbare, dirty carpet, told the same tale.
His eyes darted behind me across the path and back to the gate that barred the outside world. They narrowed again as they came back to scour me again.
"You'd better come in Blackwood". He proffered the

way with a wrinkled and pasty gnarled hand.

I turned back for a moment in hesitation. Almost a Jonathon Harker at the gate of Castle Dracul? Or simply an unsettled fellow entering the malodorous home of a mad, middle-aged man I once knew?

The interior did not disappoint. A mix of peeling wallpaper and dirty carpet that smelt of Griffith; not a pleasant smell at all.

"You came at just the time he had told me. He never lies. Come through Blackwood, come through".

Griffith folded one hand over the other, and then nodded his head toward the living room as he scurried off, his reeking, emaciated frame carrying on a dreadful dance as it clicked and scuffled its way up the ramped floor of the hall and into a side room…

I frowned and then followed.

The living room (was that term too ironic?) carried the same putrid smell; sickly and tart, almost like a negation on the nose in some way, as if someone had removed an obvious smell that was the signature. There was also a faint trace of a metallic scent combined with the predictable ammonia.

Griffith hurried to the corner of the room, near the dirty window, and began searching through a pile of papers that were stacked upon a small occasional table. The room was decorated with stacks of books and papers, most tumbled over revealing Griffith's spidery, shaky handwriting and odd glyphs and illustrations in dark inks.

He murmured to himself under his breath, occasionally his voice would crack and I would hear the sonorous sound of another, before his throat returned to whistle and wheeze.

'I am sure it is here master. I put it here. I kept it for him as you asked'.

I furrowed my eyes and glared at him. Keeping my hand firmly fixed upon one of the burgundy Chesterfield chairs, to alleviate the slight dizziness from the smell, I snapped the occasional side glance around the room.

A modern word processor was perched on another table which was placed in front of the fireplace. It was still switched on, the cursor blinking on the green screen and a few floppy disks discarded around the dirty keyboard. It must have been a trick of the light or smell that left me convinced that the two plugs that were visible, and not in their sockets, belonged to the equipment.

How else would it draw power?

"I came because of your sister, Griffith. She wants to know if you are okay", I stammered, my head was becoming increasingly fuzzy and my eyes were starting to blur.

Was it the smell? Or was it something that was cloying at my mind? Some kind of foul whisper in my consciousness?

As I moved forward a step I noticed that the floorboards beneath the carpet had a give to them, almost a spongy feel. Another footfall confirmed this. I lowered my gaze to the carpet. It was matted in a thin mould. Speckled with some sour looking patches of fluid, I shuddered to think of its origin.

Yet, why would such a modern house have floorboards? No modern houses had floorboards. My semi-addled mind blustered through my mouth. "Floorboards".

Griffith turned slowly and looked at me. His sickly grin peeled back to reveal yellowed teeth and blackened tongue.

"I have hidden knowledge and hidden things, Blackwood", he grinned again; that sickening grin.

I could no longer take it, covering my mouth I felt the egress of my brunch through my fingers as I stooped over, still holding onto the arm of the Chesterfield.

My mind was swirling to match my vision, almost like the worst vertigo I had ever experienced. Despite the shaking of my head to clear it, despite the attempts to look away I could only see his eyes. The icy, grey malignancy of his eyes. The madness that hovered at the back of them.

I rushed for the door, rebounding off the wall as I fell into the corridor, raising myself back up, unsteadily, on the gradient and clawing at the handle with violently shaking hands.

"You will be back Blackwood. I will find it for you and you will come to know", the deep, malign voice assaulted me as I threw open the door and fled from that place.

3.

The rain was hammering against the old window panes. The recent layer of gloss allowed the water leaks to run to the small pool that had gathered at the base of the window on the sill. The last resting place for a dead fly.

The hotel room was warm, heated by an old fashioned radiator and provided a comfortable haven from the weather outside, despite the eighties décor.

I sat on the bed, staring out of the window, a cup of instant coffee in one hand and my Filofax in the other.

My jacket and car keys were on the floor near the door.
I had ditched the coat and the keys with the plastic
AVIS fob as soon as I had entered the room. Perhaps as
a way of ditching the day so far.
I opened the address tab of the file on my lap and
looked at my handwritten scrawl

ANEKA GRIFFITH

Ashton's sister, and the reason I was here in this
miserable, misty place to begin with. I had planned to
spend my three weeks back in the UK catching up with
London and exploring the tea-shops and pubs of the
South Downs, not being stuck here in the rainy North
trying to reason with a madman. I had been all too keen
to be the white knight to the sister that I had a crush on
all those years ago. Now it just seemed like something
irrelevant to me.
Never mind though. I suppose, even being on the other
side of the world, there are still thighs that blind.
The phone clicked and then rang, the occasional pop
and crackle from the line.
The voice that answered was familiar. I had not heard
Aneka for almost seven years, yet still that sing song
quality of her tone rang through the telephone line.
"Hi, Aneka, it's me Blackwood."
"Ah, hi. So you made it in one piece then?"
"Yeah, Manchester's not quite as exotic as Heathrow
though. Brings back too many memories of Uni. Cold
dorms and not enough blankets."
"Not a problem for you in Oz now though Blackwood."
"Nah, well, not until winter comes, gets a bit nippy
there. Can get down to ten degrees on some nights."
"I'm sorry to impose on your holiday Blackwood. I
wouldn't have said anything if I hadn't found out you

were coming over."
Our ex university gang were thick as thieves.
"No worries Aneka. I couldn't let a mate go unhelped if I could be of some use. I called on Ashton earlier, he seemed, err, pleased to see me."
"You called? Blackwood, I told you you'd need to be accompanied by Paul and I. I think it's part of the section three that we agreed to. They were going to keep him in for a long time after his last assessment."
"I just can't imagine old Griffo being like that Aneka. I hadn't seen him since the incident so I didn't know. I mean he went to hospital after it but that was like ten years ago. I never realised he was still so hung up over it."
"Hung up? Well that's one way of putting it. The psychiatrists tell me, off the record, that if he wasn't so pumped full of **Chlorpromazine** he might do anything to hurt himself. He never leaves the house. He's in there brooding day and night. Gets some kid or someone to do his errands for him, or so he tells me. I don't know what to believe."
"I can't see some kid wanting to go anywhere near that place. It's not exactly welcoming. Anyway I spoke to him and he seems to want me to see him again."
(I gulped at the very thought).
"That's good. I thought you may have a bit more luck than we have. He can't stand Paul. He won't even open the door when he visits. I knew he'd remember you. You were such good friends at university. Before the, well, you know."
"I know."
"Did you get the bits I sent for you at the hotel? The diary and things?"

"Yes, thanks. They handed them over when I was checking in. It was all very impressive. Made me feel like some sort of undercover detective."
"Well, let's hope you can shed some light and get Ash to open his eyes. He should be in hospital not in that bungalow. I haven't the heart to force him back into the wards again. He needs to go voluntarily."
One less hassle for Aneka and Paul I presume.
"Okay Aneka, leave it with me. I'll give you a call tomorrow afternoon when I've had a squiz."
"A squiz?"
"A look, Aneka, a look."
"Oh, okay then. Bye Blackwood."
"Bye."
4.
I threw the small parcel on the bed and opened the fridge to view the mini-bar. Hardly worth the effort; two, tiny, cans of lager, two equally tiny cans of pop and a miniature of vodka. On second thoughts I was probably best sticking with the half mug of tepid coffee. It might keep my brain ticking over.
The package was wrapped in brown Manila paper and sealed neatly with tape. The handwriting seemed to be Aneka's and so, seemingly, did the wrapping. Spilling the contents onto the old patchwork bedcover revealed a few folded pieces of paper and a small, A6 sized hardcover notebook, battered at the edges and bound in some sort of yellow gaffer tape.
I set the book beside me on the pillow and glanced over the papers, they were facsimiles of a psychiatric report. The name of the psychiatrist was printed across the top of each page in a hard, capitalised style, almost as if it was there to shout at the reader for attention.

Dr Clement Johns

Odd, not the most clement of handwriting.
The handwriting seemed angry, impatient. *Another doctor with no patience.* There were edge notes scribbled in in various handwriting, each seeming to list drugs which had been tried or maybe recommended?
Pimozide 20mg, Haloperidol 15mg. Try chlorpromazine@300mg.
They were certainly feeding Griffith a few drugs up there in the Manchester mental mansion.

23/02/1986- Note, addendum to admission file. Patient Ashton Griffith brought in in semi catatonic state, on initial hygiene process patient found to have large areas of scaled tissue on rear of torso, piebald with yellow and black markings – perhaps heat trauma?
(Date unintelligible) Initial diagnosis – Paranoid schizophrenia, with symptoms of bi-polar and PTSD. Dementia praecox observed, ECT recommended for short term treatment bridging antipsychotics.
23/03/1986 - Patient often not responding to alternative therapies. Becomes withdrawn. Attacked fellow patients at hearing voices group and needed restraining at initial psychoeducation session with family.
27/03/1986 - Patient exhibiting uncharacteristic behaviour on ward. Tardive dyskinesia seems to lead to some form of chanting and spasms. Orderlies have complained of having fits of rigor (sleeplessness?) and hearing other voices beside patient's in the room.
(Date unintelligeable) Orderly found patient out of locked room and situated at rear main window in canteen. Patient remained focused on rear lawn for

twenty minutes.

04/03/1986 – Orderly reports putrid smell in patient's room and illusory experience in relation to geometry of walls. Have removed orderly from attending patient's rota in future.

07/04/1986 – Patient responding to Chlorpromazine. Restraint removed for majority of day and taking meals, liquids and exercise well.

08/04/1986 – Constant repetition of words 'Yog Sothoth' during periods of lowered lucidity. Patient nervous and reticent about discussing these words. Repetitive distressing sensation or trigger words?

14/05/1986 Patient has responded very well to addition of antidepressants, currently paroxetine, and will be recommended for discharge to his sister's custody.

Whatever had gone on between April and May in that year had certainly made an improvement to Griffith's state of mind. Whatever had happened since had, almost certainly, reversed that improvement.

I folded the papers back up and put them back into the Manilla parcel. I turned my attention to the notebook. It contained no writing on the exterior of the little tome, only various pieces of yellow fabric tape which crisscrossed the heavy card binding.

Opening the cover of the little notepad revealed a post-it note, on which was written;

'Ashton's code book – Aneka'

So, we were playing undercover detective.

The first pages of the notepad did indeed contain some form of code. Long vertical lines of random characters dropped vertically down the page in a flurry of smudged and shaky writing. The rest of the pages of the book were blank except for a couple of pages in the centre which contained some sigils and pentacles, hand drawn in red ink, seemingly from a cheap, disposable pen.

I lifted the book to my nostrils, I was correct, a faint trace of that loathsome smell again. Placing the book upon the bed I knocked it onto the floor unwittingly as I rose to make another coffee to expel the odour.

When I returned to the bed with my hot mug of black brew I had to stop to look again at the page that was open at my feet.

The book was forced open on its side, the page held open by the bottom of the door of the bedside cabinet. From where I was sitting the writing seemed obviously Griffith's. The spidery and careless hand was unmistakeable. Given the dining plate size of Ashton Griffith's hands it was obvious he had used the pages in landscape and not portrait fashion, discarding the ruled lines on each page.

Looking at the page closer it was no wonder no one else had spotted the oddity. Griffith's writing was bad enough when viewed at the correct angle but this cursive was almost impossible to read even for one who was used to it. Griffith's hand had been unsteady to say the least when this had been written.

I slurped at the coffee and grabbed my glasses from the bedside cabinet. I rarely used them, even for reading, but now I'd need their help:

> *I think it was a Saturday. I'd only gone there to*
> *help out with the tents and set up of all the gear*
> *at the camp. The experiment, with all the real*
> *technical equipment, was sited about half a mile*
> *away on the moor. I think we'd been told that the*

equipment would be powered up each night from six PM to six AM and readings would be taken every fifteen minutes.

Even back where I was I could hear the peculiar, high pitched whine of the electromagnetic resonators over the chugging of the generators. Sometimes there would be bright flashes on the moor. Mostly it was so dark that your hand was invisible in front of your face.

I think it was about three in the morning when I was awoken by a loud smash from outside the tent. The scuffling continued as I slithered from my sleeping bag and unzipped the flap of the door. I could see something moving in the dim light of the dying embers of the fire. It had tipped the table over, which was full of cooking pots, and was kicking them across the floor.

I got out of the tent and clicked on the torch. Evans, yes, it was definitely Evans. He was stooped beside the upturned table, one hand downturned like a claw and the other holding on to a small shovel. His eyes were wide and insane. His mouth hung loose and open, slowly following his head as it turned toward the light. His chest was heaving through exhaustion and his lower half was covered in wet mud from where he had staggered through the Greenfield Brook back near the experiment site.

The Land Rover behind him had received a blow across the window that had shattered the front windscreen. I looked down at the shovel in his hand as he started toward me.

I think I shouted at him, tried to tell him who I was, but he wouldn't listen. His maddened wide eyes were fixed on me, shovel raised. There was another searing light that lit up the sky across the moor, followed by a blistering crack that stunned me momentarily.

As the noise abated back to the distant rumble of the generators I saw Evans' face turn from mad rage into pitiable fear. He looked at me and then in an instant darted away into the night, heading toward the main road and Tunstead.

Another flash of light and I was up and running toward the sound of the generators. I can remember the beam of my torch looking pathetically weak in the fullness of the night there. The sky was filled with rolling cloud. I don't recall that I felt afraid. I don't recall having any emotion, as I crossed the brook and began the ascent up that hill. I could have skirted the hill and gone up the track as the others had done in their four wheel drives, but I had no concern for my aching legs nor fear of falling down that incline as I scrambled toward the summit.

As I crested the escarpment I could hear the thunder of the multiple generators as they fed the instruments whose monitors still glowed and blinked. Some of the lights were still functioning, one was flickering upon a body that lay face down and still, looking grimly odd in its waterproofs and wellingtons.

Almost as if on cue it then began to rain. I remember it so clearly. I looked up at the sky, almost as if to question the timing of this precipitation, and then I saw him.

The rolling clouds had come together, they coalesced and effervesced, inflating in soap like orbs that swelled and then lessened, like some breathing sac or bubble.

Was that an eye that regarded me, or was it some reddened pustule that floated upon that spume and scum?

Its colours waxed and waned between those I knew and those I had never seen. Maddening and horrifying.

It was enormous, monstrous. It filled my vision, taking in all of the sky and filling all of my mind with its utter disregard for both myself and everything I knew; and it knew. It knew everything.

I could feel it to my very marrow, chilling my flesh and tearing my mind.

I no longer heard generators, nor minded machine nor monitor. I heard only the silence of entropy, the deafening death of infinite space. The horror and realisation of my microbic existence, bereft of meaning, bereft of anything worth considering. A birth, life and death so sudden and instantaneous that this thing barely even contemplated me.

Yog Sothoth! YOG-SOTHOTH NAFL'FTHAGN!!! I, your servant, supplicate myself to you!

I would be forever changed, forever chained to that lurker at the threshold, the key, the shibboleth that allows the seer to glimpse the mind sundering horror and despair of the truth. To hear the insane, thin, monotonous pipes of the disharmony of the spheres, the unknowing mass that is Azathoth. The cold one, the nuclear chaos that sits beyond the angles of space.

The rest of the book seemed to describe his incarceration at Highmere hospital and his contempt for the psychiatrist that treated him, Dr Clement Johns. Oddly, it ends with the mention that Dr Johns had been asking about the diary and had been quizzing Griffith about his visions or hallucinations on the moor, in early April of 1986.

No more entries were made beside the sigils and pentacles.

I placed the book down on the bedside cabinet, took a large swig of coffee and walked to the sink to rinse my face with cold water. I felt tired, drained. Looking at my face I looked tired and drained. Almost as if the flight and the past day had aged me and taken the lustre from my usual mien; more melancholy than mirth.

If my watch was correct it was seven o'clock.

Tempus fugit.

Perhaps a few hours' sleep would restore my vigour?

5.

I dreamed of stars, of cold, dark space; empty and devoid of all reason and life. I dreamed of entropy, of heat death and the pointless slow end of all existence, tired, worn out from the meaningless struggle to maintain form and order when all about was mindless chaos.

It was of no surprise that I awoke unrefreshed. My hazy memory nagging at me that I had awoken in the night to use the toilet only to see a dimly lit figure outside the pub over the road staring at my window.

Griffith?

Did I really see that or was it a dream?

My watch told me it was past seven AM. I had slept for

over twelve hours.

Must be jetlag.

I washed and dressed and then headed down for breakfast. After a full cooked breakfast I might get my energy levels back up, plus I might also get rid of that disgusting taste in my mouth. I had naturally assumed it was a combination of Griffith's reek and my emetic escapades the day before.

I took my time at the food and allowed myself the leisure of two mugs of hot tea, more as a way of wasting an hour so I could call Aneka than anything else.

At the stroke of eight I dialled her number and waited for the answer.

"Hello?" The voice was slow and male. It was Paul, and it sounded like I'd woken him.

"Hi, it's me Blackwood. You know?"

"Err, yes. What time is it?" His tone almost sounded a little brusque.

"Eight, I thought you'd be up, sorry." Perhaps they were night owls? I knew they were both self-employed, something to do with property. Maybe they earned enough not to worry about rising early on a Thursday morning?

"No, sorry, not your fault. We didn't sleep well last night, that's all".

You and me both.

"Can I help or do you need Aneka?" Paul was obviously walking away from the bed now and lowering his voice to avoid waking his wife.

"I just wanted to know how Aneka came by the bits that were in that package, you know, the diary and the papers?"

"Ah, I think she was given them by the nurse who did the discharge for Ashton. The doctor, can't remember his name, wasn't there when we collected him. So the nurse had a look around and placed them with his other effects. Thinking about it I suppose we should've given them to Ashton but we just never got round to it I suppose".

"I think I'll have a word with the good psychiatrist if that's possible, he might have an idea why Griffith is out here in the community when he should be somewhere supervised".

"I've been saying that for years Blackwood. Good luck with that."

"I'll go there today, can you tell Aneka I called and tell ask her if we can arrange a time to go and visit Griffith, I mean Ashton, tomorrow?"

"No problem. I'll get her to call your hotel later and leave a message. You could do with one of those mobile phone things".

"I'm still getting used to these ones with a wire on. I'll see you later Paul".

I put the phone back onto the receiver and looked out of the window.

I wonder if he knows that 'see you later' in Australia doesn't imply a commitment to appearing at some point later that day?

The rain had abated by the time I got back to the room. I had a chat with the girl on the reception desk about staying on past my check out day of Monday and she confirmed that would not be a problem.

I unpacked my case, finally, and watched a little TV. Anything to waste time till nine o'clock when I could call Highmere Hospital and, hopefully, have a chat with Dr Clement Johns.

Phoning institutions is always a lesson in frustration. Most of the time it involves waiting for an aeon whilst listening to an underwater rendition of Handel's 'Water Music' or a flaky version of the Eagles' 'Hotel California'. This phone call was a little different in that I had put the receiver down and not been sure exactly what I'd been told. I had enquired about the chance of seeing Dr Johns, only to be told that I could see him between three and five PM and six till eight PM, being visiting hours he must be available then whilst his patients are receiving family members and friends.

The journey to Highmere was the usual mix of drizzle, offensive driving skills on the motorway and the inevitable wander across the outskirts of Manchester as one sign pointed in a direction to the east and another, after a short distance, back into Manchester.

Some of the signs were even overgrown with trees, rendering the whole process befuddling. Asking for directions was not advisable. The local populace were busy moving from one roof to another to escape the incessant, drenching spray that batted down from the clouds.

It was in sheets of rain and only limited visibility that I came across the sign for Highmere Psychiatric Hospital. A large, lumpen red brick structure with a few single story prefabricated buildings around it, the hospital boasted a large car park and a wealth of signage that was barely visible in the downpour.

Somehow the landscaping of the grass verges, shrubs and small trees almost told me that the place was some form of institution. Despite the best efforts of the trustees, despite being completely different to the giant,

Victorian building I was expecting, the entire place still felt like there was something unnerving about it, like a new sock upon a gangrenous foot.

It was with a little trepidation and a considerable amount of winding around the perennials and bushes that I made my way to the entrance, avoiding the path, and taking the straight route across the trimmed lawn.

I was hardly surprised by the brusque nature of the receptionist. Hospital receptionists are either born or created. One does not simply work in such a role. Their mastery of utter contempt for the visitor is only matched by their obsequiousness to their professional betters. I had assumed that most of them imagined themselves to be matrons or ward sisters, or maybe doctors. Perhaps that was why they were all so bitter? Mrs Sturgeon was no different. She spent a few minutes pretending to scan a folder full of reports that were placed on top of the large phone collection she had at her resplendent reception desk, she probably gave the cleaner one of her glares to take extra care of the laminated work surface.

I waited patiently for her to pretend to read the reports and, eventually, lift her face to acknowledge me.

"Can I help you"? She asked in a slow, clipped accent. Her eyes looked me up and down in my soaked clothes as a sour frown stretched her wrinkled mouth further down toward her chins.

I have to confess that my patience was worn a little thin, my usual phlegmatic personality had been deleteriously affected by the effects of the downpour. It was through gritted teeth that my reply emerged, the best I could do to mask my shortness of temper.

"I'd like to see Doctor Clement Johns please".

She looked at the clock on the wall to her right.
2.55PM
"Visiting hours are not until three o'clock", she pursed
her lips in a sardonic smirk.
I opened my mouth to respond, checked myself, looked
at the clock and then moved across the corridor to sit at
one of the many chairs which lined the wall. As I sat,
the first of this afternoon's visitors arrived. Some
burdened with flowers, others with fruit.
At three o'clock precisely Mrs Sturgeon lifted a small
bell and rang it twice to inform the unworthy that
visiting hours were now upon us. I caught a glimpse of
the inverted nurse's watch she bore upon her breast.
Was that a gift that had been made to her as she set
upon a medical career she never attained, or perhaps it
impressed the people on the bus on the way home?
Maybe she hoped that they might think she was a
nurse?
"Paul, can you show this gentleman to Dr Johns
please?" Mrs Sturgeon's pronunciation of 'gentleman'
was far from affirming my status as such.
Paul was a taciturn giant of a man. He looked at the
receptionist blankly, looked at me and then cocked his
head for me to follow.
I set after him, his rubber soled plastic clogs squeaking
on the polished tiled floor as my sodden jeans
squeaked along as we walked.
He stopped outside a maple coloured door with a thick
glass window stretching up above the lock. His large
open hand led my eyes up to a small plastic sign on
which was printed;
Dr Clement Johns
It was easy to see through the glass panel, beyond to

the hospital bed and the patient, sat upright and staring at the door. He was dressed in green institutional pyjamas and had a pair of slippers, a dressing gown and a bottle of energy drink assembled beside his bed. *Anyone who has slippers, a dressing gown and an energy drink is not well.*

"Dr Johns? My name's Blackwood. I just thought I'd drop by and ask you a few questions about one of your old patients"? *There is a time and a place for idle chat. I never thought a psychiatric hospital was one of them.* He looked at me blankly at first, then with a growing realisation, somehow, of who I was and who I had come to ask him about.

His eyes widened and lips pulled back in fear of me. "It's okay, I'm not here to harm you. I just want to ask you a few questions", I glanced around at the door to see if I was being watched. *Odd that they would just let a total stranger into a psychiatric unit surely?*

"I've given him everything he asked for. He's had everything. Please tell him not to come to me. Please tell him", the Doctor shivered and began to sob, pulling his covers up to his grizzled chin like an infant.

"Who is *HE*? Griffith? You mean Griffith?"

The doctor caught his breath and choked for a moment. His eyes were terrified, his lips batted at one another in an insane echolalia of that name.

"Griffith, Griffith, the Lurker… Threshold… Tome of Yussoth…Oddities of England Canaan… I got them. I stole them for him. I did as I was asked".

His shuddering hand darted from the blanket and grasped my wrist.

"He's waiting for me… Please don't let him wait for me… He can overlook me".

I looked at the door again as the patient's sobs and wails grew louder. Turning my eyes back to him I saw in his face the horror of that entity that Griffith had encountered on Saddleworth Moor. It was in the doctor's eyes, the cosmic forlornness and discouragement. The wretched terror of the unknowable and ineffable. The inevitability of that random, pointless yet painful end.

"He knows I am here… He's coming… I know he's coming here".

The patient's screams were loud now. He had let go of me and was hammering at the metal sides of the bed in blind horror and fear; face ashen and mouth distorted into a gaping maw from which various cracked screeches erupted.

It was as if he was choking in front of me.

I turned and exited the room, checking, furtively, from side to side as I left. The room was silent out here from the corridor and the slow shuffle of the medicated patients and their melancholy visitors settled my nerves as I headed for the exit.

The reception desk was vacated as I passed. No Mrs Sturgeon.

Her inverted nurse's watch was placed upon the many buttoned phone that sat at the centre of her desk though. The glass was cracked right across the face and the time had stopped at 3PM.

6.

The rain had abated by the time I had got back to the hotel. I was keen to change out of the now almost dried clothes I was wearing. A cup of hot coffee would not go amiss either.

I was stopped at the foot of the stairs by the girl on the

reception desk. There was a note for me, written in the balloon-like, teenage hand of the reception girl.

Fone cal from Anika Green. Could you call her as she like you to go with her to see her brother tonite.

I frowned at the note and turned back to look at the reception desk.

I bet Mrs Sturgeon wrote better English than that.

Trying to call Aneka was fruitless. I had tried three times in twenty minutes but the line had been busy on each occasion.

I would simply call at her home. Maybe I could give the two of them a lift. As soon as I had eaten something. I look out from the window across the road. It was convenient that there was a fish and chip shop there next to the pharmacist, it was doubly convenient that it was open for business.

I was already showered and dressed in clean, dry clothes, the almost dry clothes had been stuffed back into my suitcase. I grabbed my wallet and snatched up the bundle of keys with the small teddy bear fob and left for a portion of fish and chips that I could eat in the car on the seafront.

As I left the hotel, passing the reception desk, the girl I had spoken to earlier raised her head from her magazine as I placed my room key for storage behind the desk and bade me a barely sincere, but nonetheless formal,

"Goodbye Mr Blackwood, have a safe journey".

I looked at her for a moment and then left with no retort.

What an odd thing to say? Was it some sort of sarcastic comment?

I sat and listened to the blur of the radio, almost

inaudible over the sound of the heater in the car. The presenter was rambling on about her misspent youth in milk bars in Birmingham during the 1950s. I shook my head and switched the thing off. I preferred the sound of the sheets of rain pelting against the car's window to compete with the roar of the blowers.

I had wrapped the remains of my dinner up in the paper it came in and had tried to put it in the door well but it was full. I decided it might be best stuffed inside the glove compartment with the other rubbish, best not have half eaten chip dinners in the car when Aneka and Paul get in it.

It might ruin my cachet.

I put the car into gear and headed for Aneka's. It was quite surprising how I managed to find the place without reference to my road atlas, which was just as well as the road atlas was nowhere to be found in the car.

Maybe it got lost?

I couldn't help but grin at my own joke as I pulled up outside the empty drive of their house. It would be typical if they had gone out. At least there was a porch I could hide in to shelter from the rain whilst waiting for the door to open.

I was correct. There was no answer to my rings on the bell.

They must have left for Griffith's without me. Perhaps they had left another note at the odd reception girl's desk, telling me that they would meet me there?

The short run back to the car was enough to leave me relatively dry as I turned the car around and headed back to the North and Griffith's bungalow.

I couldn't tell if any of the houses in the street had their

lights on, the rain was too thick and too ferocious. A white brand of lighting had rent the clouded sky apart over the sea ahead. Its following rumble almost overhead.
The smell of the rain and the metallic tang of ozone was noticeable, even in the rank air of the heated car.
Griffith's bungalow was there, the messy hedges and tangled thorns lit up by another overwhelming coruscation of lightning.
There were no cars parked outside.
I stopped the car on the other side of the road and got out. The rain was hammering at me. I did not care. Leaving the gate to fall onto the path I approached the door and pushed at it. It gave freely, unlocked and unlatched.
An almighty burst of thunder shuddered about me, the windows of the house rattled as the place shook with the sound.
I left the door ajar, with no care for the rain and hail that pelted in behind me, striking at the floor and wall like tossed boulders.
"Griffith", I shouted, as I headed into the house.
The door to the living room was still open, the door next to it was closed though. A series of shifting lights came from the gaps beneath it and around it where the door had bowed and moved away from the frame.
I placed my hand upon the door and shoved, pushing the formally white portal open with ease.
The place made my head spin. It seemed to be massive. A dark, subterranean, cavernous hall or mausoleum. Whenever I looked at a part of the place, it seemed almost within reach, as if the room was the size it should be. It was only when I looked away, and saw it

in my peripheral vision, that the enormity of the place was evident.

I gasped and reached to my side for something to steady myself with, for a door frame to hold to help my balance. There was nothing. I was no longer sure where the door was, nor whether floor was ceiling or vice versa.

"You came", Griffith was there before me as I raised my head. He was adorned in purple robes now, large, malignant and somehow bursting with vitality, a far cry from the wrecked, wizened figure I had seen before. His cruel, grey eyes fixed me as I nodded.

"Yes, you were right. I'm here."

"Our master is pleased, you have done well."

"Our master is never pleased Griffith. He cares little for our stupidity. You, of all people should know that." I straightened myself up against the vertigo and dizziness I felt in that place.

The sight of my hands around the neck of Dr Clement Johns, his eyes bulging and pleading at me as I turned my head to check on the door of the hospital room. Meddling Dr Johns and his questions. The figure of that interfering crone of a hospital receptionist who had interrupted me, had persecuted me, now lying dead behind a cupboard in a storeroom.

Placing her smashed watch back upon her ever-so-important phone.

"Tying up loose ends Griffith", I grinned.

He grinned back at me and his eyes flashed as another rumble of thunder shook the room.

"I see you came here in my sister's car. Another loose end tied?" He lowered his eyes to the bunch of keys in my hand.

The back door had been open, there was a butcher's cleaver in the knife block in the kitchen. Aneka's face had been alive with confusion when I surprised her, then dead with horror as the crimson hit the curtains. *Whose sister?*
I waited for Paul when he burst through the living room door. He never even made a sound.
When I checked out of the hotel and that stupid girl said goodbye. Maybe I should have tied that loose end up too?
"Did I ever know you Griffith? Was I ever your friend?"
"I don't know. Does any of that matter now?" He seemed almost content. His face listless and blank.
"I have placed the books and the data disks you will need on the table in the living room. You must take them. This part of me is done with."
Nobody would trust an English madman, who had been in a mental hospital and had obvious bouts of insanity, on board a nuclear submarine; but they would trust a naturalised Australian maritime engineer. In twenty five years, in Hobart, when I would be called upon, I would use the arming keys, which Griffith had provided me on the floppy disks, to launch fire into the skies of Earth.
To presage the coming of our master Yog Sothoth, the lurker at the threshold, to open the gates to the Great Old Ones who would take back their place as rulers of the world. To light up the firmament to the screams of all living things. The screams of horror and despair. The power, the sheer, unbridled power.
I lunged my hands at him. He did not move to defend himself or resist. As I crushed the air from him he merely looked at me resignedly. His gnarled face once

again aged and spent. The air crackled with static, alive and bristling with energy, as Griffith's life ebbed away. As his lifeless corpse dropped to the dirty floor of that now small room I shook as I felt the eye of my master upon me.

Another loose end tied up. Now it was time to fly back across the world. Time to wait until the stars were right. Until the call came for my moment.

My moment of triumph.

Turn back the clock

It was hot, way too hot to sleep. After a few hours of lying in every configuration possible, I grabbed my bedside clock and pressed at the button to illuminate the face with the LED. It was three AM.
For someone who had spent the last few years coming to grips with the very real notion of time travel it seemed odd that the hands on a clock should seem so important.
I placed the clock back on the bedside cabinet and scratched at my shoulder, my skin was complaining in the oppressive warmth of the room. I raised myself on my elbow and lifted a curtain, the window was open as I had thought. No breeze was forthcoming through it though, yet oddly enough, now that I concentrated I could hear a faint clicking noise coming from the garden beneath my window.
Was it some insomniac cicada, scratching its legs together as I scratched my shoulders?
I moved to my hands and knees upon the hard mattress and thrust my head out of the window into that warm night air. Whilst it was dark, there were no lights other than the waning moon and stars to illuminate the lawn, there was still enough lunar luminescence to see that the garden seemed to be empty of anything to make the noise.
Still, the sound carried on, faint, yet insistent. Too random to be mechanical.
I left the bed and went into the bathroom, the call of nature overcoming whatever was calling outside.
As I returned to the bedroom the snapping noise had increased, both in rate and in racket. I thrust my head

back out the window to ascertain what was making the noise.

Nothing.

Odd, it was almost as if the noise had been coming from the paved area beneath the window?

It was as I tied the belt of my dressing gown and placed my hand on the bedroom door handle that I heard the slobbering and rasping breath of the thing that lay beyond the door, at the top of the stairs.

I could smell its infernal, sulphuric scent.

I opened the door a fraction to observe whatever was beyond it and glared eye to into its terrible face. Its eyes were alive with a mindless malignancy, wholly given to its one purpose; to hunt me, find me and then kill me. Its black body was hairless and rippled with some sort of alien musculature that seemed to twist and spiral around its thorax. Cruel canines were bared in its dripping mouth as it padded at the worn carpet, sniffing and growling.

It knew I was here, rearing back on its haunches it made ready to launch itself as I slammed the door shut. Odd though it was, I stopped for a fraction of a second and heard that clicking again. I furrowed my brows at it as the door splintered open and the creature was upon me.

As I turned and tried to leap behind the bed I knew what I had to do. I must warn myself, use the dangerous spell I had learned from that ancient, accursed book.

As the hound rent and teared I muttered the words and was gone; my body now a pulp of lacerated flesh.

In a second (or was it an aeon? I neither know nor care) I was looking up at my window. It was dark; it was three AM. I let out a silent scream at the bedroom window, nothing, a stamp of the foot, nothing. It seemed odd that I knew that a click of the fingers would work.

Had I tried it before?

I snapped my fingers together, slowly at first and then with a little more fervour.

The bedroom curtains parted and, there I was. I was sure it was me, eyes half ajar looking out across the garden.

I let out a silent scream again, only for the face to disappear from the window and the light to come one in the bathroom next door.

What was I thinking? Didn't I know what was waiting for me already at the foot of those stairs? Hunting, already aware of the unsuspecting nature of its prey.

I snapped my fingers louder now. Shouting ineffectually in accompaniment. I had to get my own attention, had to make myself aware of the only way out now.

As I heard the door splinter asunder, easily audible through the open bedroom window, I knew exactly what was taking place up there.

As I began to evanesce and dissipate my last thoughts turned to whether that spell had allowed me a chance to escape or whether that diabolical book and its dreadful hunter had tricked me into an everlasting circle; a paradox that, once started, had no end.

Pipe Dreams

Chapter One

Chris Ellis threw his superfluous jacket onto the backseat of his car and jumped behind the wheel as if he'd just won a two week luxury cruise. He hadn't; his parents had and they had texted earlier that afternoon to inform him that they just set sail for Scandinavia. He wound the window down to let in a little air; two weeks with his Mum and Dad gone from the house, it was too blissful to conceive. He had started early this morning, rising for work promptly in order to plug his X-Box into the large plasma screen in the front room (it normally sat connected to his disappointingly small TV in his bedroom).

Two weeks of gaming, interrupted by the days he had to spend in the Local Authority health department where he worked, but two weeks where he could eat what he wanted, have a beer when he wanted and next evening do it all over again.

He grinned and started up the car; an involuntary whistle passed his lips as he pulled out of the secure car park and headed off to the supermarket to stock up for his first weekend of freedom. Eight cans of beer and a few ready meals would see him through the entertainment marathon he had planned for the coming few days. Friday never felt *this* good.

As he rolled up the drive in front of the house he mused on whether to put his car in the now unused garage (his Dad's car was always parked there). It did not take a moment to realize that game time was ticking by and there really were more important things to worry about. He gathered his groceries off the back seat, closed the door and locked the car with the fob on his keychain. He left his jacket on the back seat; in this warm summer air he wouldn't be needing that.

As he strolled up to the UPVC front door that glared at him in the strong sun, something made him turn. Across the road, about a hundred feet further from the house, there was a Juvatoria PLC tanker with a pipe leading into a local drain. "Just pumping out crap", thought Chris. The lorry was glistening green, just like his dad's lawn, but it wasn't the sheen of the paintwork that drew his gaze. It was the two operators, each dressed in dark overalls with hi-vis tabards. One wore a yellow hard hat with something scrawled across the front in dark, marker pen. Both were tall, pallid, grey toned with skin that looked as if their faces were smeared with some sort of translucent oil. They both looked at him keenly; their unblinking, unemotional eyes fixed on him and unmoving. The one that was holding the pipe looked at the other in the hard hat and both resumed their job, removing their surveillance of him.

Chris assumed they were related, probably related closer than was legal. He had had a lot of experience with Juvatoria employees, most of them were picked up from the streets by that charity the company ran for employing the homeless.

The door opened with an almost audible hiss as his Dad's attempts to make the house essentially airtight proved its effectiveness again. The winter fuel bills were apparently a testimony to his father's parsimony. What was his phrase again? "Better in my pocket than Juvatoria's"; he grinned to himself, they both might be as mad as a box of frogs but he really did love his Mum and Dad.

He got in to the kitchen and placed the carrier bag with his purchases and his keys on the table. He was parched, the move from air conditioned office to the summer air left his throat as dry as his pits were wet. The beer was too warm to drink yet. He placed one can in the freezer and the rest he stood up in the fridge next to his ready meals and the labelled plastic containers of Juvatoria 'Quara' his Mum had left for him. He had half expected a sticky note on his toothbrush this morning reminding him to brush twice a day.

He grabbed a pint glass from the drainer and turned the cold tap on to full to empty out the warm water. The pipe rattled and spluttered in protest. It seemed to choke up a few drops of what almost looked like sputum and then died.

"What? Bloody stupid company", Chris' thoughts returned to the seedy looking pair outside. He tried the tap again. It shuddered but eventually a thin rusty coloured trickle turned into a torrent of bubbling, frothing water that went from warm to cool in a moment.

With his pint glass filled and a few gulps already taken
he kicked off his shoes to the corner of the hallway and
stood in front of the front room windows sipping at his
water as he looked out over the sun showered,
fenceless garden. They were still there; now both of
them were stood motionless seemingly looking straight
at him. Four emotionless, dead eyes; unrelenting, that
somehow peered and prodded through the double
glazing and net curtains to find him out.
He stepped back from the window and slurped at his
water, drops of it ran down his chin and hand. He
frowned at the two as they pulled the pipe from the
drain and coiled it around two large brackets fitted to
the side of the tanker. They appeared to be sharing a
joke and laughing. As the man wearing the hard hat
entered the cab and started the engine the other looked
back at the window, gave a humourless grin and
waved what appeared to be some finger splayed
message at him. Was it a threat? The lorry pulled away,
slowly up the road and disappeared around the corner.
Chris drained his glass and placed it on the coffee table.
"Bloody weirdos", he tugged his tee shirt from where it
was tucked into his jeans and grabbed the remote and
his X-Box controller. Flopping onto the settee he fired
up the plasma screen and console. After a brief email to
his friend from Thursday night pub meet, Neal, he
plumped up a cushion and rested his head.
"Inbred, psycho Juvatoria drainage guys or not, no one
is spoiling my weekend". He removed his socks deftly
as his other hand nimbly started up his first game on
the controller.

Within half an hour he was dead. Bent double in agony and face contorted almost to the point of no recognition. Eyes froglike, bulging; belly and torso distended and rent.

Chapter Two

Neal Quarterwaite sat back on his office chair. His dart had landed perfectly on the nose of the local MP's beaming visage that announced her intention of, 'getting us earning again'. Considering the MP's business proclivities and expenses claims it was all Neal could do to hold back a hearty laugh.

He had been Chief Editor of the Globe now for almost a year. Considering he was the only employee the title was a little grand. It did not stop him using it when it was profitable though. He had enjoyed a few free dinners and even more free drinks thanks to his press badge and elevated status.

His accession to such a lofty station in his chosen profession of journalism was due more to his disregard for digging dirt than any duty to professionalism. He had been placed in his position, and given reasonable remuneration, by the new owners of the newspaper Frank and Patricia Rummage. Frank and Pat had inherited a not inconsiderable sum from Frank's father on the proviso that they maintain his pride and joy, the Globe newspaper.

They had achieved this by employing Neal Quarterwaite; it had taken some searching to find the perfect candidate. Someone who would not go out to make a fuss or start prying into affairs that would cause trouble for the new owners, but also someone who could keep the newspaper barely interesting enough that advertisers would still use it and keep the thing afloat, well, just about afloat at least.

Neal had been the perfect choice.

Quarterwaite looked at the clock, five to nine, early again. It must be something about Monday mornings he hefted the second half of his 'Quara' all-day breakfast sandwich and guzzled at it as he slurped at his energy drink in the other hand. It was hard to believe that the sausage and egg on the sandwich were made by some sort of vegetable matter that was processed at a Juvatoria plant not that far away.
Almost home grown.
A small trumpet fanfare erupted from his PC as it came to life and presented him with his log in screen. It was picture of him and four of the lads from the Thursday night pub meet. Great times, great times.
He placed his sandwich down next to the half assembled Frankenstein's monster figurine that had sat on his desk for weeks now (a semi-wanted Christmas present). Between checking his online auctions and playing spider solitaire he just never seemed to have time to build the figurine.
His calendar flashed up;
MASY STARTS TODAY 9AM
He'd forgotten about that. Masy, the niece of the Globe's new owners, was a student at some god-forsaken red brick, pseudo-educational institution in the midlands. She was apparently studying journalism and would be spending her holiday break making Neal's life a nightmare by asking stupid questions and no doubt interfering with his meticulously balanced schedule.
Bet she has dyed red hair, a nose ring, thick rimmed glasses and sixteen lace-hole boots.
The door opened.

Neal had been wrong. Her hair was dyed bright purple not red.

Masy thundered into the room, her brows furrowed in a cocktail of incredulity, bewilderment and contempt.

"Where do I sit?" She cast her hand to the side as if to brush away the parochial nature of the small office.

"A chair might be an ideal place to start?" Neal pointed at the old, metal tubed school chair that faced a yellowed CRT monitor and a map of the area with a dart stuck in the Irish Sea.

She sat down, petulantly, dropping her leather briefcase onto the desk with a light clatter.

"Before we start I'd better make myself clear, I don't take any micro-aggressions from patriarchal tossers like you. Get it?"

Neal raised his eyebrows.

"So it's, Masy. Is that short for Mavis?"

"Margaret", she scowled.

"Ah, so your name is Margaret Mint then, eh?" Neal looked at the screen with her details listed in his calendar.

"Masy Mint", her croaking, vocal fry voice snapped at him.

"Can I call you Minty?"

"That's not my name".

"Nor's Masy", he said. A small grin emerging on his well-groomed, whiskered face.

She turned away from him and began to search through the desk drawers, eager to ignore him.

The next few weeks would take a long time to pass.

Or so he believed.

Chapter Three

Neal had not heard the ping of his email notification, it was only when he returned to the screen and saw the small envelope icon that he opened his mail client and slurped at his energy drink again.

The communication was from his friend, Chris Ellis. It was titled;

IMPORTANT

Chris had a tendency to overinflate things. To Neal it was a corollary of attending food hygiene inspections and scouring kitchen floors for mouse droppings. To anyone that does that for a living the smallest of minutiae must seem overwhelmingly important. Neal shuddered to think what Chris would make of the carpet in this office as he scraped a smattering of breadcrumbs off the edge of his desk.

As the email opened he peered over the top of his monitor at Ms. Mint. She was looking out of the window and drumming her fingers on the desk. Perhaps she was bored? Perhaps not? She would have to get used to playing spider solitaire; that is what journalism is all about at a newspaper like The Globe.

> *Neal*
>
> *I've got some right tasty stuff on Juvatoria's local factory if you're interested. Get on over to mine this weekend and we'll go over the printouts. It could make the Globe into a household name, LOL.*

That sounded suspiciously like work. He looked at the time on the email, Friday, 16:55.

Who on earth works at that time on a Friday? I'll bet Minty does.

He peered over the monitor again. She was picking bits of chipboard out of the wallpaper. He doubted she would last the day.

With some clearing of the throat and a considerable blustering of breath Neal picked up the 'phone and speed dialed Chris's work number (all ten speed dial entries were set to his friends' various locations).

"Hi, yes. I'd like to speak to Chris Ellis at environmental health please. No problem. Thanks".

He held on as the telephone now began to tell him how great the local council were whilst he waited.

"Yes. Ah, he's not in? He's not ill is he? No it's okay. I'll get back to him. Thanks. Bye".

Neal put the receiver down and stood up.

He took a comb from the pocket of his red flannel shirt and stepped over to the wall mirror grooming his waxed hair and then combing his impressive brown beard. With a slight alteration of his braces and a wink at himself he turned and looked down at Ms. Mint.

"I'm off out for a 'mo, don't do anything I wouldn't do". He grinned.

"What? Like work?" she replied, flatly.

"If you see any then report it at once and don't go near it. That stuff's a killer".

He locked his PC, closed the door and shook his head. *What an idiot.*

The dark country music seemed at odds with the seventies estate in which Chris and his parents resided. Neal turned off the radio as he pulled up outside. The estate was always silent on a weekday, it was almost as if it had a wall around it.

Chris's car was parked outside, Neal assumed that he was sleeping off a hangover after having a whole weekend free of his parents. Not very good that he never got an invite to the party though.

With a quick rap on the door and a glimpse at the
blinds still open on the front room window Neal was
ready to leave. It was only when he looked down and
saw that the front door lock had been forced open that
he turned around and looked down each end of the
road.
This didn't look good.
He opened the door and crept in. A faltering cry to his
friend rattling in his dry throat as he stepped into the
living room.
The smell was appalling. A heaving mix of mould and
the cold steel of blood, combined with the damp
atmosphere it left Neal with a balking, mouth covering
repulsion.
His friend was clearly visible, burst open, upon the
settee. Neal winced and turned his face away in
disgust.
It was obvious that someone had rifled through the
room, drawers were scattered across the floor, the
many DVDs that were usually stacked along the wall
shelves were now scattered everywhere.
The scene was overwhelming.
Neal burst back out of the house drawing deep breaths
in a horrified panic. Stabbing at his car keys to unlock
his car, with shaking and uncertain hands.
He closed the door quietly behind him and went to his
desk. After a long gulp of energy drink from shaking
hands he looked around the office. It was only when
the toilet flushed and Masy came back into the room he
realised that she had been absent.
It was fortunate that she had not seen his condition.
The energy drink had steeled him a little and he was
able to cover the worst of his nerves.

He hid behind his monitor for a moment as he opened his mail client back up and stared at Chris's email;
…and we'll go over the printouts…
He sent the email from work. He must have printed out the documents there and brought them home with him. That would mean that the originals were possibly still at his desk?
"How do you fancy a trip to the Council's environmental team offices, Minty"?
"Masy", she retorted.
"Is that like maybe"? Somehow his reply seemed a little flippant to him, under the circumstances.
"It's got to be better than sitting in this dump", she gathered her student accessories and followed him from the office and to his car.
Neal held in his nerves and tried to strengthen his wavering lower lip. He felt nauseous with fear; a grinding dread that made him wish he could return to the morning's start and wisely stay in bed. He could not face venturing out alone. At least Ms. Mint was some form of safety in numbers.

Chapter Four

It was with some renewed confidence that Neal closed his car door and straightened the collar on his shirt. Somehow his sense of journalistic integrity had been pricked by his friend's death and the subsequent rifling of his house.

Neal would find what Chris had been investigating, report the matter to the police and then allow them to pursue the matter from there. It was really quite astounding how stoic he was being, considering the shock he had been presented with. He raised himself up an inch as he strode up the entrance to the local council offices, Minty in tow, her large boots stomping at the steps.

With a cursory nod to young Kylie on the reception desk, Neal was a regular visitor to his friend in the environmental health department, he made his way behind the customer service desks and into through the faux maple door that led to the inner workings of the local council. Chris's desk, and the office of environmental health, was the first side door on the left; fortunately, saving a friend from having to brave the bureaucratic bowels of the borough council.

He opened the door and slipped easily onto an office chair immediately to his right. Swinging his feet beneath the desk with considerable experience.

"What are we doing here, if you don't mind me asking'? Masy looked around the windowless, open plan fluorescent lit office. A civil servant peered around his desk divider to look at her with considerable confusion. She scowled at him through her clear lensed spectacles. He retreated back behind his carpet covered shield.

"I'm beginning to ask myself that". He rummaged through the stacks of paper on Chris's desk.
"There might be a story in it and a whole lot more". As Neal glanced over the monitor in front of him he noticed two figures had entered the office from the opposite door. They flashed police warrant cards at one of the environmental officers and began asking a few questions. As they followed the pointing civil servants finger to the Chris's desk Neal ducked and came face to face with the plastic cactus desk toy on Chris's desk. They were gone when the detectives began impounding the computer equipment and hard files from Chris' desk. They took almost everything.
It seemed odd to Neal that the local police would be so quick to follow the trails that he had taken. It was only through a thorough knowledge of how scrupulous Chris was that Neal had presumed to search his work cubicle first. Surely the police would be more concerned with searching the house and notifying the parents etc.
As his car crept past his old friend's house he noticed that nothing had changed. The door was still seemingly closed, the car was still parked on the drive. He was certain no one had been at the house since he had left. That could only mean that the police, or whoever they were, had gone straight to Chris's desk in the hope of finding some sort of information. Presumably because they were all too aware that Chris was no longer among the living.
That familiar, worried sickening feeling came over him again as he pulled up outside the newspaper office.

"I think you better tell me what's going on here. You look like you're about to faint". Masy took another energy drink from the fridge and handed it to him. She was right, he did feel a little light headed.

He outlined as much as he could piece together of that morning's happenings before Masy interrupted the silent mulling.

"In that case we had better call the… Oh, hang on…" She looked at the plastic cactus which was now sat upon Neal's desk as it had sat upon his friend's.

"Why did you take this?" She picked up the ornament.

"He used to bang on about that thing every time I visited him at work. It's a data stick. The top comes of the thing to go into a USB slot on your PC."

Masy took the top off the USB drive and placed it into the computer on the desk. It took a little while for the creaking PC to read the USB stick but eventually a new window open and displayed the content of the drive. A collection of text files and images all with the word;

'JUVATORIA'

Included in the file name.

Neal looked down at the screen again and winced. He really did not like where this was heading.

The majority of the documents were pieces of interviews with contractors that had worked around Juvatoria's plants in the past, delivery drivers, IT staff, building workers and so on. It was testimony to Chris's single minded purpose that he had traced these people and quizzed them on the issue.

The majority had reported on the cult-like behaviour of the company and its employees; many of whom were from Juvatoria's social welfare program 'New Chance', which took the homeless from the streets and offered them paid employment.

Stories of the regime that the new employees underwent, many of them belittling, some of them humiliating or even dangerous, predominated. There were also reports which emphasised the secrecy of what was contained in the large chemical silos at Juvatoria's plants. Aspersions as to the cleanliness of the company's food preparation regime and the safety of its biofuel division rated high too.

There were also two invites to an open day at the local plant, dated for the following day, and a letter of introduction from the head of customer relations Deborah Moteck.

"Well, that settles it. We're investigating the local Juvatoria factory tomorrow then", Masy turned her dissatisfied frown towards him.

"What's this 'we' you're referring to?" said Neal.

"I'm here to learn journalism. I didn't think I'd actually get a chance to do some in this fleapit, so I'm not missing this chance. Plus, don't forget that my Aunty and Uncle own this rag, when I graduate I'll probably be your boss." She smirked at him sardonically.

Neal realised his opportunity to kick the next phase in this nightmare into the long grass had just disappeared. He had planned to tell Masy he was going alone, spend the day at home with his phone switched off and then come in the next day with reports of a day spent at a totally wholesome and above board Juvatoria plant. No such luck.

"I'm off home now. I'll see you bright and early at nine tomorrow for the open day. Oh, and don't forget you won't need a packed lunch. It'll probably be free food", she hefted her bag and stomped out of the office.

Neal looked down at the 'Quara' all-day breakfast sandwich's remains. Pushing it away he turned to look at the open documents on the monitor.

He felt sick. A mixture of textured vegetable protein, fear, energy drinks and trepidation combined with the plague of butterflies in his stomach to render him almost nauseous.

There had to be a way to get out of this.

Chapter Five

Neal's car pulled up outside the office at twenty past eight. She was already there. His sleepless night had afforded him no inspiration to create an excuse for missing today. In fact it had left him simply more compliant to go along with what appeared to be a fated event.

The idea that his friend might still be sprawled out on the settee with his chest burst open made the entire train of events seem somehow unreal; leaving Quarterwaite with the impression that he was merely a detached observer somehow.

Masy slammed the car door as she settled into the passenger seat.

Five feet of fury.

He had to wonder why she was continually angry, she had received everything she had ever asked for. Maybe that was the problem? The world was rarely as generous as one's doting parents.

The half hour drive was devoid of conversation. The banging dance music that came from the stereo made sure of that.

As the car pulled into the car park Neal rubbed at his face and eyes with his hand and puffed out a long breath.

"Are you sure you want to do this?" He was as much asking himself as he was his passenger.

"Getting cold feet at the last minute? How typically male." Masy got out, sans her bag, just clutching at her phone and a notepad and pen.

Neal muttered obscenities under his breath as he exited the car and led the way to the security station that blocked entrance to the site. A small queue of suited officials and minor local dignitaries were huddled around the building chatting and jostling for recognition of their authority.

Most would have been smoking and attempting to digest their breakfast in his Dad's generation, now though they stood together in small groups bad-mouthing their fellow employees, some stood on their own, awkward, kicking the kerb or pretending to read important messages on their phone.

Eventually the small group was filtered through the security hut and visitor badges were supplied to those who handed over their introductory letters.

"Chris Ellis?" The security guard looked Masy up and down. "You're from the council's environmental health team?"

Masy glared at him through her unnecessary spectacles.

"Chris… It's short for Christine?" She wrinkled her nose at him and snorted.

The guard was utterly emotionless. His dead eyes merely looked at her in neutrality. It almost seemed as if he had fallen asleep with his eyes open.

A colleague moved behind him and whispered something into his ear. The guard nodded a tiny tilt of the head in assent and handed Masy her visitor badge.

As Neal moved to the front of the desk he could feel the full flush of his bright red face. His hands were trembling and his throat was cracked dry.

The guard looked at him, then at Masy and then finally handed him a badge too, merely writing something he could not see on the base of the introductory letter. Masy brought her phone up to take a snapshot of the security room for posterity.

"No photos!" It was the man that had whispered into the security guard's ear.

"We have a lot of very sensitive corporate research in this plant. I would be grateful to the party if everyone could refrain from using all phones and other devices while we are on the tour. We have a lot of competitors who would be very interested in what you are about to see". The man grinned. Neal could imagine him wiping the spittle from the corners of his mouth afterwards, he was so overly obsequious.

The small group was ushered out of the hut and into the wide road that ran down the middle of the processing plant. On each side a mass of convoluted pipes twisted between giant silos, some white and some silver. Here and there small huts were placed, dwarfed by the industrial containers that surrounded them. From these huts scuttled the various workers of the plant. All wearing the green overalls bearing the Juvatoria name and black safety helmets and protective boots.

Every worker seemed to carry that same hollowed out, disinterested frown upon their faces. Exactly the same as the security guard's face that they had just been past in the hut.

The tour guide set off at a slow pace and the group followed behind. Neal and Masy fitting into a gap in the middle as the rear of the group was covered by two of the company's security guards who pressed the visitors forward to maintain a tidy formation.

The group was hastened along the main road past the busy maintenance workers, all outfitted in the identical uniform of black and green. They laboured in complete silence, each disregarding the other and seemingly unaware of the group of strangers that passed them by.

"As you can see our workers are totally committed to their tasks. We have a saying here that 'chat is for breaks'. All unnecessary communication is kept to a minimum to improve concentration on the task at hand".

The small company continued, snaking their way through the worm casts of pipes that went from the ground in tangles and led away in every direction.

"So we have seen a small area of our storage and filtration units, our system allows for this area to syphon off the protein residue of our process which is then used to make our various meat substitute products. I am sure you have all enjoyed a Quara ham sandwich before eh?"

The guests nodded fervently and muttered to one another, mainly in anticipation of free food.

Of course we also create the waste filtration systems on the other side of the plant, which is a similar process. Those systems are sent across the continent via our dedicated rail platform which is just visible over there.

He pointed to the large marshalling area where a long line of flatbed carriages were lined up behind a modern locomotive, each containing a huge tanker held in place by heavy steel clamps.

"Isn't it dangerous having waste filtration and food made at the same place?" The interlocutor was a small man, a fiercely pressed, badly fitting suit hung around him like the drapes around a budgie's cage.

"Well, all our produce is created under hermetic conditions. Both our food and filtration products amount to pellet form at this stage of the process. Plus, you will find that the waste filtration product is actually sterile upon it creation. Our attention to detail is quite meticulous".

"And what about industrial accidents? How come we have no record of any industrial accidents on your sites?" The man pressed on with his questions, his face becoming ruddy with ire.

"I am not aware of any accidents on our sites which would warrant reporting"

"I have it on good authority that you are lying, and that not only do you cover up accidents at these sites but you even have medical stations to treat the injuries so that no one ever hears about them. Like that one there". The man stabbed his forefinger at a small hut that was positioned a hundred yards or so ahead. It bore a green on black caduceus plaque beside its door.

The short man set off at an alarmingly fast pace toward the hut which left the tour guide stunned momentarily. After a moment he flashed his now angry eyes back toward the two security guards at the rear of the party and signalled with a nod for the guards to set after the sprinting man.

As the rest of the party clamoured forward to press for the best view of the pursuit the guide lost control of the situation and was jostled about at the front of the scrum.

Masy darted from the back of the group with a pinch on Quarterwaite's arm and disappeared into the knots of thick, steel piping. Neal followed after her, not even thinking about his subterfuge as he watched the chase unfold further up the road.

There were a series of shouts from near the targeted hut, followed by a shrill referee's whistle. The sound of the tour guide's exasperated voice shouting into his transceiver was accompanied by a loud alarm sounding and a dull, monotone voice announcing over still air of the plant that all members of the party should reassemble at the guide's location.

Neal looked back as he pressed on, following the pipes deep into the processing area. It seems that they weren't the only ones to leave the group then.

It was only at that moment he realised what he had done. He had simply wandered away from the guide without even thinking about it.

He shook his head as he pressed on behind his placement student.

"What on earth do you think you'll find doing this? It's not like they'll have a map posted up showing the location of a secret documents building or something is it? We could even get arrested for this".

"Some journalist you are. Pathetic". She scrunched up her nose at him again in contempt.

"I'm a journalist with a job, not a journalist in jail, I..."
Neal stopped as a green Juvatoria minibus pulled up
outside one of the buildings next to their hidden
viewpoint. The driver of the vehicle and his passenger,
both clad in green overalls and now wearing what
looked like black riot helmets, chest protectors and
knee pads emerged and spoke with their compatriots
that had emerged from the building.
"Get the processing units inside, site maintenance go to
the induction building. Quickly".
The command prompted swift action. The formerly
homeless occupants of the van were paraded out
speedily; three of the ten, notable for their height and
build, were guided away by one of the employees who
had recently emerged from the building. The others,
two of whom looked emaciated and in need of medical
treatment, were guided inside the building by the
remaining green overalled Juvatoria workers.
"When do we get our meal? I was told we'd get a
meal?" The speaker was a thin man with a broad Irish
accent.
"We'll get you cleaned up first, then you'll get fed,
watered and have a clean change of clothes". The
worker's voice was robotic, monotone. He placed his
hand firmly on the man's back and guided him into the
building.
"Induction building? I wonder what happens there."
Masy followed the course of the small party as they
walked away from the van and headed back toward the
main gate.

"If we're going to get caught trespassing then we might as well do it in the Processing building. That sounds like it's the place where all the action happens". Neal crept from behind the pipes which were hiding him, slid around the minibus and opened the large door slightly to peer inside.

"If I didn't know better I'd think you have go a backbone after all", said Masy.

The pair crept into the building, the strong smell of chlorine and the oppressive heat and humidity resembled a swimming baths. The tiled floors and painted walls added to the impression.

A short corridor led to a set of double doors ahead, the place was brightly lit by spot lamps in the ceiling, despite the heat and humidity somehow the place felt cold, at least it did to Neal's backbone.

The double doors were made of wood with a maple veneer. Long brushed steel handles and small mottled and meshed safety glass windows sat aside each other in the centre of each door.

Opening one of the doors and inch allowed Neal to see into the next corridor, over to his right there stood a large metal, freestanding cupboard, on the opposite side of the space was a long window which led to a smaller maple door. At the far end of the bright, tiled corridor were a pair of doors identical to the ones he was behind.

"Let's get behind that cupboard and have a look what's going on", he nodded to where the large metal object would provide a foot and a half of cover to anyone standing at the end of it.

Masy nodded, still not forcing a grin, and headed off to the back of the cupboard, brushing past him as she did so.

If Quarterwaite had been reluctant to enter the corridor it no longer showed, thanks mainly to Masy's further contempt for his circumspection. He joined her and peered through the window from behind the cupboard. The only thing that was visible was sprays of water occasionally hitting the window and the resulting shadows cast on the internal wall by the powerful lighting.

Masy moved forward to have a closer look at the window just as its accompanying door opened inward. She darted back behind the cupboard as a line of naked, soaking wet and hunched new arrivals were moved along the line from the water room to the double doors. After a brief moment the lead employee opened the doors and firmly ushered the trembling line of soaked, skinny men into the room. The final Juvatoria employee turned to look back down the corridor through the visor of his black helmet. The two interlopers pressed back against the wall behind the cupboard. Staying there until the far doors closed with a dull clatter.

It was Masy who peered around the cupboard first, she turned back to Neal who was looking at the corridor in confusion.

"Something's not right about this place", he nodded at the wet room surreptitiously.

Masy scrunched her nose up again and shook her head.

The pair set off toward the double doors in tandem, reaching them together and both grabbing at the same handle at the same time. Neal waved his hand for Masy to open the door and she pulled gently at the handle enough to allow a clear view into the room.

The area was dark except for a highly illuminated central area that had the appearance of a circus ring or small theatre. Rows of solid wooden seating ran around the central stage in three arcs. In the very centre of the illuminated area a tall, wiry man was busy poring over the controls of a small brass or copper panel that was mounted on top of a riveted glass and metal frame. He was wearing green scrubs, a green apron and a dark green surgical facemask.

Behind him were eight cylindrical pods, made of the same brass and glass riveted construction as his small panel. They tapered to the top like odd, mechanical flower buds.

The seven men huddled together in the centre of the circle, covering themselves as best they could and eyeing each other nervously.

"I'll be giving each of you a shot now, make sure you aren't bringing any nasty bugs into our nice clean plant, eh?" His voice was not hollow like his fellow employees, in fact it seemed to drip a smarmy condescension which was alarmingly close to that of the tour guide they had heard earlier.

As the man turned to a small table that was at the back of his control panel Neal and Masy slipped through the door and hid behind the rear rows of seating. Considering the lack of illumination they were all but invisible. It gave them something of a sense of relief as the guards at the back of the naked men had an odd habit of turning around to look at the entrance to the room.

The man turned back with a large kidney tray containing a number of syringes. It was hard, from the distance, to tell exactly what was in them but it was obvious that they were made of the same brass like metal and glass used in the other items in the room. The masked man began to inject his subjects in the upper arm, rubbing each fresh piercing with a small swab of cotton wool.

The sixth man in the line, the same Irish man that had asked about the meal earlier, was not as phlegmatic as his colleagues. He backed away at the sight of the syringe.

"You're not sticking that effin' thing in my arm", he pulled back away from the threat and backed into one of the security guards.

The helmeted guard grabbed the man's arms and wrenched them tight behind the Irish man's back. The syringe shot forth in an instant with no regard for finding a vein or ensuring minimal damage to the flesh. As the Irish man was released to clutch at his arm and bend over in a show of humiliation and shock, the last man was similarly handled by the guard and the masked man stabbed the last syringe into the unwilling recipient's arm.

"Get the ungrateful sods into the chambers", the
masked man nodded over at the pods and pulled at a
small lever to open the clamshell doors upward.
The naked men were bundled in by the security
guards. The Irishman and the last man to be injected
putting up some resistance but eventually succumbing.
The last man to be placed inside his pod asked meekly;
"Will it hurt"?
The guards ignored him and closed the door.
The hidden watchers exchanged glances as the masked
man drummed his fingers on the brass instrument
panel. Occasionally he would push at a lever that
would amplify the heavy breathing coming from one of
the pods. As the first cries of discomfort came through
the crackling speakers he turned to his guards, clicked
his fingers and dismissed them to exit through the
double doors. Masy and Neal did not flinch as they
passed, completely oblivious as to their observers.
The first cries of complaint against the fire that had
been pumped into their veins came from the two near
starved men. They howled in pain and dropped to their
feet, one ramming his bulging eyes against the glass as
the flesh of his face bubbled and blistered.
Soon the screams erupted from all the pods, the
Irishman pounding at the door in a tortured blend of
agony and rage. Their exposed flesh was clearly
becoming loose, amorphous even. It pulsated as the
sizzling blood was pumped about beneath it. Some
writhed on the base of the pods others scratched at the
doors, in bursts of shuddering torment.
The meek man who had entered the pods last had had
his answer. He screamed at the man in the surgical
mask;

"What did you do?"
The masked man responded with the press of a button
to open the microphone to the pods.
"You were losers in life, now you'll be given a chance
to give back what you took out. Why do you cry? You
should be happy you are going on this adventure. The
pain will last for a few moments that's all".
He lowered the speaker outputs as the tumult of
agonised misery reached its crescendo. The subject's
limbs hung loose; their bodies had blistered and
inflated into hideous blasphemies of humanoid shape.
Ever increasing in size as the lungs of the subjects
collapsed, as eyes simply dropped out of expanded
sockets, as gigantic, pustule tongues lolled from
drooped bucket like mouths. Soon no discernible limbs
were apparent, just a nebulous mass of pallid skin like
matter, that trailed a bile-like slime across the glass
doors, as it continued to expand to fill the now
vanishing space in the pods.
With a nonchalant press of a button there was a soft
sound of compressed air and the containers were
drained of their foul matter. The entire mass was
sucked up into the pipes that sat above the pods and
was compressed into one writhing form as it was
extracted into the large main pipe that exited the back
of the room. The occasional clatter of unmodified bone
clattering at the pipe's sides as it left.
Within seconds the room was completely silent, the
doors to the pods were reopened as the masked man
pressed a button on the console and a sickly smell of
emulsified fat and bodily fluids lurched across the
miniature amphitheatre.

As the man walked behind the pods and exited from a door Neal turned to Masy, her eyes wide open in horror and her body shaking in revulsion. He tried to speak but could not. For once words had failed him.

Chapter Six

They left the room through the barely concealed fire door behind them. It was with a surreptitious glance that Neal had poked his head out of the emergency door and winced at the bright light outside. The area was clear and their exit from the building went unnoticed as they darted back into the relative safety of the many pipes that led from silo to silo.

"What the hell are we going to do now?" Masy, for once, looked unsure, perhaps even fearful.

"Get out of this bloody place A.S.A.P", for once Neal did not expect any disagreement.

"We're not going to get out of the main entrance unnoticed so I reckon our best bet is to get to a bit of fence or something, where we can sneak under it. Just as long as we keep clear of those guards", Quarterwaite gave an involuntary shudder. He hoped she had not noticed.

"What about them?" Masy pointed over to the edge of one of the silos where a small, white 360 degree visibility camera was attached to a horizontal bar.

"Bugger", he set off at a cautious pace along the walls of narrow pipes.

"A large silver pipe painted with a single green line along its middle followed the way they were headed and disappeared into an imposing looking building which was only partially visible through the tangle of pipes that hid them.

Masy turned her head to the building they had just vacated.

"That pipe with the green stripe is the one that runs into the building with those glass cage things", she winced and shivered at the thought.

Neal followed the pipe with eyes and silently stared at the large building it led to.

"Have you noticed how quiet it is? No alarms, no people, not even a bird twittering?" Quarterwaite raised his palm as if to present the atmosphere to his colleague.

"Let's have a look at that building and then get out of here", Masy was beginning to lose her fearless façade. The pair crept along the line of the pipes, eyes darting about and a constant watch made for the ever present CCTV cameras. It was only a matter of a few minutes before they had followed the large pipe to where it entered the substantial, concrete faced, cream building; a faint whirring sound and several clangs of metal against metal from within the building broke the nervy silence.

Perhaps it was some sort of break time? There had to be a reason why the place was so quiet.

On the far side of the large pipe there was an opening into the building which was covered by loose bands of vertically suspended opaque plastic strips, presumably to allow fork lifts and similar vehicles to pass in and out. They approached the entrance with circumspection, each checking in every direction as the crept along the edge of the wall.

Neal glanced inside and was greeted by the sight of a cavernous factory interior, rows of conveyor belts were lined up along the base of the interior and where flanked by enormous cylinders which gave the occasional nearly inaudible hiss of some sort of pressure release, the walls of the factory were a mass of gangways, ladders and odd looking instrument panels of glass and brass. There were no employees to be seen at all. The lines of conveyors were still, Boxes were stacked, seemingly in mid transit. The whole place almost seemed to be frozen in time.

Quarterwaite gestured with his head and entered the building Masy followed after him, making sure they were not observed from outside. It was obvious that a thorough view of the entire building could be had from one the metal walkways that framed the walls so it was Masy who made her way up the ladder as Neal eventually caught on and followed her up, after spending a few moments looking at the odd artifice of the technology on display. It looked archaic and yet almost alien. Something about its shapes and hues reminded him of old fashioned desk lamps and Edwardian tales of fantastic worlds and time machines. They crept along the checker plate walkway silently, stopping to look at the various consoles with their dials metered out in odd numerals that neither had ever seen before. More pipes ran hither and thither, sometimes turning abruptly and running across the path as if their placement had been put there before the gangway or perhaps even in spite of the gangway; *by something that needed no brass footpath to access those consoles?*

They clambered down another ladder to attain a wider
metal balcony that overlooked the main floor of the
factory area, it allowed a glimpse of just how large this
entire place was. The many processing tanks sat around
the edge of the factory like massive metal monoliths,
their wide, open glass windows filled with frothing,
foaming emerald matter that glistened in arrays of
glints like oily froth on putrid water.
It was unfortunate that their new viewpoint also
allowed the three guards that were staring at them
from the floor below a fine vantage too.
It was with no noise but a great deal of haste that the
three green overalled and black helmeted guards
launched themselves at the ladder that led up to the
balcony and began scrambling after the unwelcome
visitors.
Neal had switched into automatic as soon as he saws
the guards below him, he did not even think as he
backed into the dark niche between two consoles and
wedged himself behind a number of pipes. Masy
responded to the clatter of the guards on the ladder
with shock. She looked around for her accomplice to no
avail, dropped her things and then sprinted along the
metal gangway and straight into a line of pipes that
blocked any further movement away from her
pursuers.
She looked down at the drop from the walkway she
was on. It was about thirty feet to the floor. It was
doubtful she would make the drop without injury, even
with her sturdy boots. She looked back around just as a
guard lashed out at her with a small cosh and struck
her sharply across the back of her head leaving her
dazed.

As the guards dragged her away screaming, Neal grabbed at a pipe to steady himself as he sobbed silently and heaved at the air for breath, his entire body wracked in fear.

"Neal, Neal where are you?" Her voice was pleading and confused.

She let out a scream as the sound of someone tumbling down metal stairs and being followed by guards, in sturdy boots of their own, assaulted his ears.

"Neal… Please…"

He dropped onto the floor, sliding down the side of a console and still hidden behind the pipes, silent tears of terror ran down his trembling cheeks as his wide eyes darted for a glimpse of what was occurring beyond his hiding place.

"Neal"…

It seemed like he had sat there for an age, choking disgust at himself mixed with drying tears of fears stilled for the time being. It was only as he focused on the situation around him that he noticed Masy's phone was lying right in front of him on the checkered brass plate of the floor. It was so incongruent with the surroundings, it might as well be a belisha beacon with accompanying pole. He moved his foot out of the hiding place and hooked the phone, pulling it back towards him.

The thing was silver and expensive, one of the latest models. His shaking hands grabbed at the thing and he barely managed to keep hold of it as he lifted it to look at the screen. With a press of the power button the screen illuminated and presented an unlocked interface. He could call the police, make them aware of what was happening here? No, the police had been at Chris' office, they hadn't even been at the site of his murder.

That all seemed so long ago now.

As he pressed the thing to his forehead and closed his eyes it buzzed and let forward a raucous rendition of the emotional dribblings of some mawkish pop teen idol or other. Neal glared at the thing.

AUNTY PAT CALLING

He stabbed at the receive call button, anything to quieten the ear splitting din that the thing was making.

"Hello?" He whispered; lifting the phone to his ear, his voice cracked with fear.

"Neal, darling. Where are you?" The voice sounded familiar, overly familiar.

"Who, who is..?"

"It's me, darling. Pat Rummage, your employer?" The voice immediately recognisable now.

"Where are you?"

"I'm in the Juvatoria Plant, in the Juvatoria factory. You won't believe what they…"

"I know you're there, but *whereabouts* are you?"

Neal pulled the phone away from his ear and stared at it. How did she know he was there?

He tossed the phone across the balcony and heard it clatter, then shatter, upon the concrete floor below.

The sound of the people entering the factory floor stunned him. There were a few of them at least. A small hiatus was followed by the sound of machinery starting into action. The solitary voice he could hear was a voice that chilled him; the masked man from the auditorium. "Neal, there's no point hiding up there. We know where you are now".
Neal cowered into a ball, placing hands over his eyes and mewing quietly;
"No, no, no"
"Come down Neal, don't make us come and get you".
Neal crawled from behind the pipes and raised himself to a stooped, shivering wreck.
"It was Masy, she wanted to come here. I never saw anything." He stumbled toward the stairs sobbing. The warm damp patch of his fear expanding across the front of his trousers.
They were there waiting for him. The masked man and his guards.
He climbed down the stairs gripping onto the rails tightly, each step leaden and horrible.
"It's Masy you want. Take her, she's the one that saw everything. Do it to her, not me"
"Too late to plead for that now Neal, look", the masked man offered a hand toward the nearby moving conveyor belt where newly formed pellets of Quara nuggets were being fed out of an automated hopper, here and there a bone or skull fragment would appear amongst them. Yet, then, something black, black and round.
Masy's unnecessary spectacles. They trundled down the conveyor with the rest of her, at least he assumed it was her.

Neal caterwauled and lunged back, into the ready
hands of the guards.
"We'll ask our benefactors what is to be done with
you" said the masked man.
As Neal screamed at the sight of the conveyor, he lifted
his head at the sound of buzzing; noisy, insect-like
buzzing, and stared into the giant compound eye of a
hovering thing.
"Our benefactors" The masked man said flatly.
Neal's screams faded into madness.

Chapter Seven
He sat at the desk. His back straight and his cap set at a perfect angle to cover his shaved head and the large surgical scar and stitches that stretched across the back of his crown. His eyes were blank.
Chat is for breaks
He lifted his head from the screen in front of him and stared at the man in front of him nonplussed.
"Neal, it's Pete, I've taken over your old job at the paper. I found the notes you got off Chris Ellis about this place. Dynamite. Are you still investigating? Can we meet up at lunch time or something? Go over a few things"
Neal looked at the man blankly for a moment and then clicked the mouse pointer on the **SECURITY ALERT** button on his desktop. Within seconds he was joined by a number of guards in the security hut. The guards dragged the man away from the Juvatoria entrance and up towards processing as he shouted and bawled protests.
Our benefactors.
He maintained his silent stare at the wall.